PANDORA'S BOX

Alice Thompson

THE ECCO PRESS

First published in Great Britain in 1998 by Little, Brown and Company

THE ECCO PRESS
100 West Broad Street
Hopewell, New Jersey 08525

Printed in the United States of America

Acknowledgements
p. vii-viii: Lines 57-101 from *Works and Days* by Hesiod,
translated by H. G. Evelyn-White,
Loeb Classical Library, Cambridge, 1950.

Library of Congress Cataloging-in-Publication Data

Thompson, Alice.
Pandora's box / Alice Thompson.
p.   cm.
ISBN 0-88001-670-1
I. Title.
PR6070.H6578P36   1999
823'.914—dc21   98-37076
CIP

9 8 7 6 5 4 3 2 1

FIRST EDITION 1999

PANDORA'S BOX

To my mother and father
and to Stephen

'**B**ut I will give men as the price for fire an evil thing in which they may all be glad of heart while they embrace their own destruction.'

So said the father of men and gods and laughed aloud. And he bade famous Hephaestus make haste and mix earth with water and to put in it the voice and strength of humankind, and fashion a sweet, lovely maiden-shape, like to the immortal goddesses in face; and Athene to teach her needlework and the weaving of the varied web; and golden Aphrodite to shed grace upon her head and cruel longing and cares that weary the limbs. And he charged Hermes the guide, the slayer of Argus, to put in her a shameless mind and a deceitful nature.

So he ordered. And they obeyed the lord Zeus the son of Cronos. And he called this woman Pandora, because all they who dwelt on Olympus gave each a gift, a plague to men who eat bread.

But when he had finished the sheer, hopeless snare, the Father sent glorious Argus-Slayer, the swift messenger of the gods, to take it to Epimetheus as a gift. And Epimetheus did not think on what Prometheus had said to him, bidding him never take a gift of Olympian Zeus, but to send it back for fear it might prove to be something harmful to men. But he took the gift, and afterwards, when the evil thing was already his, he understood.

For ere this the tribes of men lived on earth remote and free from ills and hard toil and heavy sicknesses which bring the Fates upon men; for in misery men grow old quickly. But the woman took off the great lid of the jar with her hands and scattered all these and her thought caused sorrow and mischief to men. Only Hope remained there in an unbreakable home within under the rim of the jar, and did not fly out at the door; for ere that, the lid of the jar stopped her, by the will of Aegis-holding Zeus who gathers the clouds.

Hesiod

PANDORA'S BOX

PANDORA

'do not be afraid of what you want'

One night Noah was dreaming when the sound of hammering at his door woke him up and he immediately forgot his dream. He put on his dressing-gown and barefoot walked down the stairs of his house into the darkness. The carpet was soft beneath his feet, like the fur of an animal. The glass cupola above the hallway was being hammered by a thunderstorm and at first he thought it was just the sound of the rain that had woken him. A flash of lightning crossed the glass above, cracking the sky in half and illuminating the darkness inside, but there was a hammering on the front door that was louder than the storm, so he opened it.

Flames were licking the edges of the sky in front of him and it took him a moment to realise that there was a fire burning on the doorstep of his home. It took him a further moment to make out the shape of a shadowy figure standing in the midst of the flames, making a star pattern with its limbs. Noah went into the flames to pull the figure out, without hesitating, but the flames were cool and did not burn him. The body he brought out was so charred he could not tell whether it was a man or a woman. He extinguished the flames with his own body.

The hospital stood on the top of the hill like a monastery and he drove the still breathing body, in his car, up the road that wound up like a snake from the town below. The rain lashed on to the windscreen and the lights from his headlamps were reflected in the flooded road. As Noah approached his destination, the whiteness of the clean-lined and rectangular hospital glimmered above him in the headlights, untouched by the storm that raged around it. He drove up the hospital's straight gravel path made of silver-grey shards of granite, past the flat lawn cut in a square on either side.

Leaping out of the car, Noah ran, as if straight through the glass of the glass doors that opened silently and discreetly before him, into the empty hospital corridor.

The mechanics of Casualty took over and he was not needed for the moment, except to say that there was a burnt woman in his car, that no, he did not know what the cause of the flames were or how the patient had got on to his doorstep; and he drove back down the hill, his car empty, listening to the sound of the windscreen wipers on the glass. He felt tired, as if he had risked too much.

He stayed awake that night unable to get the image of the burning woman out of his mind. The intensity of the flames flickered through his memory, her silhouette more like the shadow of someone real than someone real, within the flames. He could still hear the terrible silence, except for the beating of the flames, in the night air. He could find no metaphor for her. She was just an image imprinted on his retina, like the reflection of the outside world in the pupil of an eye.

Dr Noah Close worked at that private hospital as a doctor, specialising in the reconstruction of human bodies. The hospital was usually a calm place and when Noah entered it the following morning, a sense of serenity came over him. Its organisation and complexity reminded him of the human body, but of an idealised body that never broke down, a body that was infallible. The smell of the hospital was bleached and anaesthetised. The scents of the body, of sweat or excreta had been emptied out. There was no hint of mortality here for there were very few deaths. People came here to improve on their bodies, not to leave them behind.

Everything was always silent in the hospital, except for the sound of metal clanging together like the ringing of bells in church. The corridors went on for miles, so polished that the walls and floors reflected Noah back. The wards were half full of patients silently waiting to be rebuilt.

A few minutes after Noah had arrived at the hospital, the consultant called him into her room, to discuss the patient he had brought in the night before.

'We still haven't managed to find out anything more about her, Noah. She hasn't regained consciousness and no one has reported her missing. To be frank, it's a miracle she's still alive. I've never seen anyone survive such extensive burns. Nor do we have any idea what actually caused the burns. The burns don't seem to have destroyed the skin tissue in the normal way. The surface of the skin has disappeared in patterns that are almost symmetrical.'

'And we have no biographical information about her at all?'

'No. So there's no photograph on which to base a reconstruction of her. The surgeon who took her on would have *carte blanche*.'

'I don't think I can do it.' He had understood what she was saying.

The consultant looked at Noah, surprised that he was refusing. She noticed that even though he appeared very calm and certain he was gripping his hands together.

'Why not, Noah?'

'You're offering her to me because you think the chances of her dying are high. Which they are. Her whole body requires massive reconstruction. She'd be a guinea pig. Even if she did survive, we'd be condemning her to a life of pain. I would be afraid of giving her a life that she might not want.'

'That's not the reason you don't want to do it. And you know it. This is a test of all your skills and resources as a surgeon. And you're scared of failing.'

'It would be better to let her die,' he repeated.

After work he returned home only to sleep and dream. His home was decorated in the white and chrome minimalism of the hospital. His work was his life and because he dreamt in a place similar to the hospital, his work seemed to be his dreams too. He knew just before he fell asleep, in his heart, what he was frightened of, that this strange woman was his dream come true.

The next day he told the consultant that he would take on the woman as his patient. She had already been shifted to a part of an empty hospital ward where the curtains around her were perpetually closed, like a bird's broken wings. Nurses and consultants over the next few weeks bustled in and out at regular intervals like the toy men and women in weather houses, but Dr Close who was attending another case, and at the same time waiting for her to recover sufficiently for him to start work on her, would not see her again until a month later.

During that month of waiting for her, he thought little of her, and she did not impinge on his waking life. He walked down the ward past the closed curtains around her bed without turning his head. He had helped heal burn victims of all ages, mended their skin, disguised their scars, but never one with burns of such magnitude. He had reserved her for the future.

At the end of the month the curtains were pulled back. She was wrapped up in bandages, the white soft cotton cocooning her raw limbs in criss-crosses across her body, a jigsaw of lines overlapping each other. She looked like an alien being. She lay absolutely still, spread-eagled out in the shape of a star. The view from her bed looked out on the smart driveway and tidy lawn but the tiny slits in the bandages would have limited her vision to the white ceiling above.

Because of her stillness, when Noah sat on the edge of the bed to make his first close examination, he thought she was still unconscious. However, he caught a glimpse of movement in her eyes, between the bandages, and realised the reason that she was not moving was because it hurt to move. The space between her limbs had become precious. He had grown accustomed to the power of fire and its legacy, but the pain of his patients was of a dimension he could not, saw no point in, imagining.

He carefully removed the bandage from her hand, which revealed a melt-down of tissue. He was unsurprised to find her skin still raw but was bewildered by the way the burns had marked her skin in odd spiral shapes, more like the prints of a huge godlike hand than random marks, as if the flames had had fingers which had held her tight. He could see right through the spirals to her veins and the intricate workings of the inside of her body, through to the lines of muscle and fragile bone. He asked her to move the fingers of her right hand which she did as if she were playing a run of notes quickly on a musical instrument. He watched the tendons stretch and relax. Some patches of skin on her wrist remained strangely perfect like patches of snow. He was struck by how soft the skin was, like a baby's, recently made. However, the ratio of unburnt skin to burnt was so small he could not really understand why she was still alive.

The hospital had still not managed to make a positive identification. Noah concluded, because her vocal chords had remained miraculously unharmed, that her sustained silence was due to the profound emotional trauma she had experienced.

Noah tried talking to her, but she refused to reply. He tried to find out where she had come from, how she had appeared on his doorstep, but her eyes just stared resolutely up through her mask. However, the fact that she said nothing made it easier for him to concentrate, as it was what he could do with her body that interested him. Her body was his project. It was a challenge for him to work with such raw material, to edit, to create, to build upon.

He had to restore skin, using prostheses, inch by inch, regrafting a foot as if traversing a desert. Her body became a landscape over which he had to cross, but he saw it in terms of square inches. The limitations of the future lay within the circumference of his immediate world. He took on her body a moment at a time. He was remoulding her not with the touch of human flesh but with the caress of the knife, the prick of the needle – medical science had become an act of love.

Noah worshipped the body, had studied all his young adult life its nerve endings, its intricate complexities, the way the brain fired up. Part of this worship involved the need to understand its workings, to be able to understand it through its mechanisms. The body was his faith. He was an atheist, but he understood why Christians ate the body of Christ and drank his blood. He understood the importance of flesh and bone.

Every day, he would bring her flowers for the vase that stood on the table beside her bed. He did not do this for her sake but because of his own need to alleviate the sense of absence he felt when he was working on her. During the day it was very bright in the room, that clinical brightness that reminded Noah not of the piercing light of the sun, but of the mysterious luminosity of the moon.

She lay still, wrapped in bandages apart from the section Noah was studying, as if unaware of his attentions. She was like a stone goddess being worshipped by a pagan, anointed and bathed, offered sacrifices, but always remaining impassive.

Noah worked methodically, skilfully, but the healing process of her body staggered his belief. He had never seen anything like it. He uncovered her foot only a day after he had operated, and was shocked by the speed and success with which her undamaged skin had melted and merged into the grafted skin. The apparent line between the two had completely dissolved. It was as if the parts of the body he had touched had never been licked by the flames at all.

While operating on her foot, Noah had discovered both her feet had six toes. He had considered an amputation of the redundant toes, to align her balance, but had found the bone strangely resilient. He decided to leave the feet as they were.

As her skin healed she also began to move, her slight stirrings reminding him of the beginning of spring. First of all she moved her hands and feet and then her arm but her head remained perfectly still. When her right hand had absolutely healed he gave her a piece of paper and pen. Without moving her head from its position of staring at the ceiling, her blind hand quickly and expertly moved over the paper lying on her stomach. She handed him back a perfect representation of her right hand.

That night he sat on the edge of her bed and took her now healed soft white hand and held it in his own. The hospital had its own rhythms and, like a body, never shut down, even when apparently sleeping. In the soft light of the hospital at night, the bandages smoothed out her body like stone. The shadows showed up the faint lines between the rolls of bandage like the veins of marble.

'You are a gift from the gods,' he said to her sleeping body.

Noah's look was very still until something struck his attention, then he looked as if what he had seen had brushed up against him softly and suddenly. His eyes were violet blue. His body had a heaviness about it, as if slightly melted down. Above all, his surface value was of ordinariness. He did not seem on the face of things, on the surface, particularly interesting. When it rained, however, the water caused the dark strands of his hair to stick to his face like question marks.

Noah was in love with the empirical world. The physicality of the world, the building blocks of cities, as well as the rhythms of the natural world, offered him constant pleasure. In spite of the obsession he had for his work, Noah was not unaware of the seasons changing outside the hospital and he appreciated the mechanics of the world as he did the mechanics of the body. He didn't need an imagination as the world was mysterious enough for him.

Even though Noah had a sense of wonder for reality, he was always certain that if he collected enough information he could get to the bottom of the wonder. Just as every time Noah built up the body, dealt in its physical realities, he felt in some way he might get to the bottom of the mystery of what it was to be human. His life ran in a straight line from beginning to end and he walked along it, unaware of the drop on either side.

In his bedroom, a photograph of the Hale-Bopp comet was pinned to his wall. Late at night, he would get into bed and continue reading from his collection of encyclopaedia, pleased that he had reached a new letter before falling asleep. The facts of the world were like jewels he collected. He did not bother to thread the facts together, he just piled them up like a magpie piled up pieces of silver foil in its nest.

Noah had decided to leave the operations on the patient's face until last. For he knew that the face would prove the most challenging part of her body to regraft. While the rest of her body continued to heal wondrously quickly and perfectly, her head remained bandaged up. Her face had been so badly burnt that there was nothing of the original structure left. He would have to rebuild the bones themselves.

Noah started to draw diagrams and work out the measurements of the reconstruction. Using a textbook photograph of an idealised woman's face, he set out a face on paper of symmetrical proportions. He would give her a model face. He realised the overlying result would still look like a raw concertina of scars and blemishes but at least he could give her face's basic structure a proportion that bore some underlying semblance to perfection.

Reconstructing her face took many weeks of painstaking operations. A few weeks after surgery Noah bent down over his patient's head to unravel the bandages. Her eyes just flickered from between the swathing, as his hands expertly and slowly pulled off the fabric. He could not stop his heart beating more quickly than usual. The result would be a testament to all his powers.

But he could not believe his eyes when he saw what his hands were gradually revealing to him. Appearing beneath the bandages, inch by inch, was a beautiful young woman's face, a face so white and soft that the skin seemed as if it had never seen the light of day. This was not a face that had been so badly disfigured its features had been unrecognisable. It was a face that was the exact replica of the textbook photograph upon which Noah had based his structural measurements.

Her cool, pale, reflective eyes looked at him, in the same speculative trance with which she had stared at the ceiling all these months. She still hadn't uttered a word. What kind of woman was she? he thought. That night he dreamt of her decapitated head floating down a river, her mouth opening and shutting singing voicelessly.

The next morning he told the matron to fetch the patient some clothes and discharge her immediately. Noah wanted nothing more to do with this aberration of nature. Later that afternoon, when he walked past her bed, it was empty, the white sheet pulled tightly back over the grey blanket, the regulatory six inches, smooth and flat.

Although he had dedicated himself intensively and over a period of time to only one patient, he did not miss her, as might have been expected. On the contrary, he was relieved that she had gone. At first, Noah had been pleased by the initial speed of her body's recovery, which he took as a reflection of his medical powers. It was only when her recovery ran against all Noah's notion of what was possible, that he began to feel disturbed.

He kept his own private fears to himself – she had been his patient and no one else's, and he alone felt responsible for her. After all, it was his doorstep that she had landed on. He felt her recovery was all part of her inexplicable appearance outside his home, something peculiarly specific to him and he wanted to forget all about it. A few doctors had remarked to him on her uncanny recovery and then, as completely as she was healed, she was as completely forgotten.

Noah returned to his work on other patients, shortening noses, enlarging breasts and using prostheses to replace amputated limbs. But it was noticed in the hospital that since the arrival and departure of the anonymous patient something about Noah had changed. It was difficult to pinpoint. Something to do with the way he walked, the way he talked. He was slightly more vehement, as a character slightly less controlled, but it was barely perceptible.

Noah did not expect to see her again. Nor did he wish to. He had the rest of his life to be getting on with. Noah's world was certain and complete. His new patients slotted into this world like pieces into a jigsaw.

Noah lived in his house on his own and was protective of his space, so he couldn't understand why, one morning when he walked into his dining-room, he became overwhelmed by the sensation that someone had just left the room. As he was not superstitious and unused to a feeling based on an irrational belief he quickly forgot the impression that had seemed so real at the time.

A few days later, opening the door to go to work, he looked down to see that a present, exquisitely wrapped in paper as sheer as ice and tied with satin bows, was sitting on his doorstep. He ripped open the paper to find, nestling inside a tiny cardboard box and wrapped in cotton wool, a little glass nightingale. That evening, he put the glass bird on the fire and watched it melt and flare-up and split open.

More than a week later, after a very exhausting day at the hospital, Noah was walking up the path to his front door when he saw, through the ground-floor window, someone stand up from the table where he or she had been sitting and walk slowly out of the dining-room. He just saw the dark outline of a figure and could not tell whether it was a man or a woman. Trembling, he quickly unlocked the front door and, turning on the lights, searched the house but found no one.

It was exactly a month after Noah had discharged the patient from the hospital that he woke early in the morning to hear a sound which he could not place. Lying awake in bed, listening hard, he managed to place the resonance – it was the strain of a harp. The composition of the music was not of a type he had heard before, for the music did not have an obvious melodic line nor even a recognisable rhythm. Nor could he place it in time.

At first the noise annoyed him by keeping him awake, so, in order to stop up his ears, he put his pillow over his head. But to his surprise, he could still hear the harp clearly, the music seeming to reach into his room, through the crevices, on air currents, rather than through solid walls, until, every time he fell asleep again, it slipped back into his dreams.

In desperation, he rose, put on his dressing-gown and went out on to the landing. The music seemed to be coming from the spare bedroom and he followed the music through into the room. He was faced with the back of a woman sitting on a chair. She was playing a harp. He could only see the back of her long golden hair as her hands manipulated the strings.

Part of him wanted to shout *What in god's name are you doing in my house?* but another part of him wanted to approach her and touch her arm to see if she were real. Before he could do anything at all, the woman, who had obviously heard him enter the room, stopped playing and turned round to smile at him. He did not feel so much scared as tentative, wondering why this was happening to him, why she had insisted on coming into his life again after he had already healed her once. What was it about him that she could not leave alone?

'What are you doing here?' he asked her, gently. He could not help noticing how milky white her skin was, how disturbingly perfect.

But still she would not use her voice.

She took out a piece of paper from her pocket and gave it to him. On it she had written *Don't you realise how much you need me?*

She stood up and walked towards him and embraced

him and he buried his head in her shoulders. He could smell all of her, the smell of hope and possibility, the smell of the future. She had come up to meet the rapture inside of him. He wanted to wring the rapture out of his own accord and offer it to her as sacrifice.

She came into his life and filled it with bliss. He could hardly believe what had happened. She did not need to change the severe geometry of his house or alter the blankness of the walls. Her presence was enough to transform his clinical space into a palace. He kept on putting out his hand to hold her arm.

'You'll never leave me. You'll never leave me.

And she would shake her head, mouth never.

Words were no longer an issue. She had come out of the blue, pulled apart the sky like a curtain and stepped out on to the stage of his life. All he could do was give silent applause for this clue to his life. He had been given a clue to his life.

That she was mute only appealed to his sense of justice. For how could someone who appeared to him so full of wisdom be cursed with words? He never wondered about it – that she came to him with no friends, no family, no history. He felt instead gratitude towards her for the absence of her past. Her blankness offered him relief. He liked the idea that he had created her, forged her out of fire. Her smell, her limbs, her smile were what counted, were what added up to her. He chose to deliberately forget what he did not know. He called her his wife. He called her Pandora.

That Pandora could not speak never seemed to perturb her. She did not seem to have the need for communication at all. She was self-contained. It was not that she did not observe, it was simply that she had no need to express her observations. She only revealed herself in the embroidery of tiny flowers, which seemed to him to reflect her interest in the small details of life. Even her body language was silent. She walked softly, as if she did not want to take up his aural space.

One evening, Noah was rummaging at the back of their bedroom cupboard looking for a lost shoe when he felt a sudden pain in his finger, as if someone had bitten it. He brought his hand out quickly – a cut had seared its tip, a drop of blood swelling out of his skin. Putting his hand back into the cupboard more cautiously he brought out what had cut him, a box he had never seen before, made out of opaque glass, its edges cut to a fine edge, fine enough to draw blood easily. The box had a criss-cross of iron bars webbing it, and a butterfly clasp for a lock. Noah tried to open it, but it was locked tight. He shook the box but whatever was inside made no noise.

Noah had discovered the only possession Pandora owned. She had obviously not wanted him to find it. He returned it to its hiding-place. It was part of his deliberate forgetting that she had a past at all, that allowed him to forget about the box as well.

Noah wanted to buy Pandora, his new wife, a small wedding present. As he was passing one of the shop windows in the village, an array of glass animals, including a nightingale, caught his eye. Remembering about his burning of the gift of the glass bird that he had assumed Pandora had left on his doorstep, he went into the shop to buy one for her.

The door gave a soft tinkle as it opened, and Noah climbed down a steep step into a small, dusty shop, with antique plates, teapots and china pug dogs crammed on its shelves. The only light in the shop came from the small display window that peered up into the street.

The antique seller sat behind a desk at the door, polishing what looked to Noah suspiciously like a crystal ball, until he drew nearer and saw that it was a paperweight. The man had a face turned in on itself, like a gnome, the hardness of his eyes at odds with the twinkly smile that beamed at Noah over gingery whiskers.

'I would like the glass nightingale in the window, please,' Noah said.

'What is it about those nightingales?' the man said. 'That's the second one I've sold in the past couple of months.'

Noah was just about to tell him that the person who had bought the other one must have been his wife, when the man continued, 'To a most peculiar man. At first I thought it was a woman. Very beautiful. In the classical way. But when I looked harder at the face, I could see that it was a man. The features seemed to dissolve in front of me, as he stood. A very intense-looking person. As if he was trying to break out of himself, if that makes sense.'

It didn't make sense to Noah, and he asked the man to wrap the bird up, as it was a present for his wife.

'A lovely present, that will be. But very fragile. Be careful not to break it on the way home.'

When Pandora opened the box to pull out the glass bird, he was so taken aback by the pleasure on her face that he vowed to buy her others. Soon she had a collection of animals which she separated off from the rest of the house by a glass case. It stood in the centre of their drawing-room.

The swans, pigs and ducks were all in transparent glass, except for the dashes of colours in their eyes and tails. Every day she would take them out of their case and clean them with cotton wool and water. He knew that he was not allowed to touch them, instinctively.

Sometimes he saw her when she thought he wasn't looking, bring them gently up to her face, stroke them and kiss them with her lips. The cold glass would leave small imprints on her cheek of the animal's outline, before the blood suffused her cheek again.

When he looked at her in repose, he became convinced that she too was made of glass, like the glass case, that he could see straight through her. Inside there was a part of herself she retained, she kept safe and to herself, which she would never let out, like one of the glass animals, forged by fire, that stood in the glass case and refracted the light. He thought she was too fragile for this world, and that in this world he should not touch her in case he should break her.

He began to feel like opening the box hidden in their cupboard. Or breaking it.

Noah began to grow curious, curious about Pandora's secrets. He wanted to know what went on inside her head, gain access to her thoughts. He began not to be able to accept her separateness. He had dreams at night that she could talk, that in fact she had been able to talk all the time, that she was telling him that she could speak all these words, and the words fell out of her mouth like jewels and scattered across the floor, falling in crevices. He knelt down on the ground and scrabbled for them desperately in the dust.

But the more he started to ask questions about her past the more distant she became, and this turned into a kind of nightmare for him, to have this beautiful female in his home, to be breathing her air, smelling her scent, yet not to know her mind.

They made love in a series of gestures like a deaf and dumb language which had ceased to have meaning.

On the day of their first wedding anniversary the first letter arrived. It was addressed to Pandora. It was her secret smile as she read it, which struck Noah foremost. Every morning, for a week, a letter in the same handwriting would arrive, and Pandora, as she read it, would give the same smile. Give was the wrong word for that smile, for rather it took something away. She would leave the letters propped up on the mantelpiece, behind the carriage clock.

Noah refrained from asking what the letters said or who they were from. His curiosity about his wife had grown so strong, he felt there was a danger now in articulating it. On the seventh morning, after she had left the room, Noah went into the drawing-room and plucked out a letter from one of the seven envelopes. Written on the fine paper in blood-red ink capitals was DO NOT BE AFRAID OF WHAT YOU WANT. Noah plucked another letter out from an envelope to read the same words. Every letter contained the same message, written in the same way, positioned on the page identically. It was impossible to distinguish between them. Noah ripped the letters up.

The letters continued to arrive and Noah continued to rip them up. Pandora started to wash herself incessantly and take baths that would last an afternoon. She would lie in the bath until the water turned cold and her flesh turned purple and she cried out with the pain of her body turning into stone.

Even in the middle of the night, while Noah lay motionless beneath the sheets, he would hear her rise quietly from the bed. He would listen as she walked down the corridor into the bathroom and turned on the taps, listen to the sound of running water filling up the bath.

She began to turn away from his advances in bed, as if his touch might leave dirty marks on her she would be unable to remove.

She became reluctant to leave the house now, even on

her own, and grew idle indoors. Noah not only worked, he did the business of sustaining their lives, cooking, the housework, shopping. He did not realise that she was not frightened to go outside but frightened that if she did, she would miss an opportunity of watching the letter land on the mat, miss opening it instead of him, miss reading the words DO NOT BE AFRAID OF WHAT YOU WANT.

It was Noah who became scared when he left home for work and left her behind. Frightened that she would disappear as strangely as she had arrived. As he went to the hospital and operated on bodies, pulled skin over wounds, he felt as if he were trying to heal a wound in himself. For his love for her had made him fragile, cut him open so his heart showed. He worked even more intensely, confident that if he could just heal enough bodies he himself would become healed. He realised that this was the sacrifice he had made, that having once been strong he was now weak.

Pandora started to embroider a tapestry which was on a grander scale to the ones she had sewn before. Her needle and thread darted across the blank canvas and while her head was bent down, her eyes narrowly focused on the small stitches, Noah saw, with a mixture of love and despair, that whatever Pandora set her hand to she did perfectly. She was, like her name, all gifted.

At first he thought that her design, like all her previous tapestries which now adorned the house, was purely decorative: plants were appearing in the margin in intricate patterns. But as she continued to sew, he saw that these patterns only formed the border. A story was beginning to take place in the centre of the canvas.

A landscape appeared of cliffs and a blue sea with little white tips like crescent moons. The trees were small and crouched, oranges and lemon balls heavily hanging from their branches. The scene was like the backdrop of a classical Greek mosaic in the colours of the bright yellow, whites and blue of the Mediterranean.

Outside, in the village that Noah and Pandora lived in, it continued to rain.

The story became more complicated as background figures appeared, playing in a distant field. Stitch by stitch the large figure of a beautiful, naked woman with full breasts and wide hips filled up the foreground. Her face remained blank.

A few days later Noah went into the dining-room where Pandora normally left the tapestry propped up on its easel. To his surprise, Pandora had covered it with a white sheet. Curious to see the work, Noah lifted up the sheet, and with his eyes followed the gentle fluid curves of the stitched woman, skin the colour of snow. But to his shock, he saw that Pandora had added on to the faceless woman's pubic area a huge phallus, surrounded by coarse, dark, pubic hair, each hair beautifully stitched, the tip of the erect penis stitched soft as red velvet.

Then, as suddenly as the letters had begun, the letters stopped. Weeks passed of silence and Pandora slowly began to recover. He could see her start to blossom again, begin to participate again in their shared world. It was just when Noah thought everything was back to normal, when everything seemed all right, that it finally fell apart. Just when life had slipped back into place, when life had started to reflect back what it was supposed to be.

Looking back afterwards, he remembered what they say; that the deceived in some way want to be deceived. They are in some blunt way asking for it. Being deceived by another goes hand in hand with deceiving oneself and that is what the deceivers manipulate – the desire to deceive oneself, contrary to all the evidence. Hard evidence that sticks out like rock, evidence that can break bones.

Since Pandora had become his wife, Noah had made sure that he returned home at the same time each evening. But that evening he had had to stay behind at the hospital to help a colleague. This had delayed his return by a few hours, and arriving home Noah was surprised to find the house already in darkness. He assumed that Pandora had gone to bed, that she had taken an early night. Otherwise Noah saw nothing in the house out of the ordinary, nothing to make him wonder.

He opened the door and walked into the dark hallway. Not wanting to wake her, he did not call out her name as he usually did. Normally on hearing her name she would immediately appear round a corner but that night, because he did not call her name, she did not appear.

He went into the bedroom. She was lying in bed, her back to him and, deciding not to rouse her, he shut the door quietly behind him again and went into the kitchen to get something to eat. He then went back through to the living-room and switched on the television. He woke up in darkness in front of the empty flickering screen. Returning to the bedroom, he undressed in the darkness and having climbed into bed beside her, promptly fell asleep.

In the dead of night, for no reason, he woke up. Feeling unexpectedly aroused Noah turned to his sleeping wife and began slowly to caress her smooth and pliant back. He moved his hand slowly round to touch the dry, white flesh of her breast but his hand met with a sticky warmth that caked her skin. She was oddly motionless. Curious, he flung back the cover just as the moon came out from behind the clouds. Leaning over, he saw that her whole front was congealed in blood. Her breasts had been cut off. Blood also ran over and between her legs on to the sheet, staining the bed.

He tried to shake her like a doll, back into life. It was to him as if someone else was screaming, an animal sound, not real, until language took over, started to hammer inside his head a single word over and over again, in the silence, NO, NO, NO. Her unseeing open eyes simply stared at him, impassively.

Covered in her blood, he dialled the emergency number but when the emergency services answered Noah found he could not say anything, he had lost the power of speech. He put the receiver back down. He dressed over his blood-stained body and ran out into the street but the streets were empty and the windows and doors remained shut. He returned slowly to his house and shut the door behind him.

He was surprised, when five minutes later the doorbell rang and he went to open the door, to see a policeman standing there. Noah looked at the policeman, standing on the doorstep, and wondered where he had come from.

The policeman knew of Dr Close's reputation as a cour-teous, skilled doctor, much respected in the community, even if he and his wife very much kept themselves to themselves, and so he had acted promptly after tracing the source of the emergency call. This was a small, peaceful village and he was not used to anything much out of the ordinary. The policeman looked down at the doctor's hands.

It was all going according to some plan, Noah thought, this is what policemen were supposed to look like. He felt now oddly calm and became certain that because this middle-aged man was bulky, with a red face and slow manner, he was an actor in police uniform, going through the motions, and that this wasn't, after all, happening in real life.

The policeman entered the house and began a search while Noah waited for him in the kitchen. The policeman returned more quickly than he had expected, as if he had jumped a frame.

'What have you done with the body, doctor?' The policeman asked.

Noah nodded. Of course there wasn't a body. It had been some kind of hallucination. Pandora hadn't died at all. He followed the policeman back up the stairs into the bedroom, but was puzzled when he saw his own bloody fingerprints on the white walls where he must have put his hands coming down. Standing in the doorway of the bedroom, Noah peered over the policeman's shoulder on which, he noticed, flecks of dandruff were lying.

The bed was empty. Her body had disappeared. However, there were still bloodstains covering the sheets blossoming out, crushed and carnal.

The policeman had turned round and was staring at him intently, and Noah looked back at him, bemused. Noah understood immediately that he had to be the first suspect, husbands always were, but he still felt nothing, could think only in terms of recognising what was happening, as if it had happened before, but in the realm of his imagination. He became confused between his memory and the present. None of this was real to him, by any means – after all, in some way his life was now only half an hour old.

The police station was in the centre of the village, a Victorian redbrick building, and Noah was glad as he walked up its steps that it was still night so that there was no one on the streets to recognise him. The policeman took him into a small, brown, shabby room with a low, teak table piled high with magazines such as *Life* and *Time* and locked the door behind him. As Noah sat down in one of the faded armchairs, the room's smell of must and wood polish struck him.

An hour later, the door opened again and a tall man in plain clothes, whose face had been cut from a series of acute angles, entered. As he pulled up a chair to sit opposite Noah, Noah looked into his serious eyes and felt the sudden desire to confide in him.

'My wife,' Noah said, 'has been murdered. He's taken the body.'

'He?'

'The person who killed her.'

'You saw him?' His voice was unexpectedly gentle.

'No.'

'So why did you say he?'

Noah hesitated. 'I just took it for granted . . .

'It's best in these cases to take nothing for granted.'

It never ceased to amaze Noah how expressions could transform a face, physically seem to change its shape. Suddenly the detective's distinct face altered, as anger disjointed its angular appearance until it seemed lightweight and impressionable.

'Can you tell us a bit about your wife, Dr Close? Is there anything in her history or recent past which would lead you to think that someone might want to take her life?'

Noah thought, he was trying to think clearly in this situation. 'There were letters. But they had stopped.'

'Letters?'

'Anonymous. Addressed to Pandora. They always said the same thing: DO NOT BE AFRAID OF WHAT YOU WANT.'

'I beg your pardon?' The detective looked insulted, thinking that Noah was addressing him personally.

'That is what the letters kept on saying. DO NOT BE AFRAID OF WHAT YOU WANT.'

'Have you still got them?'

'I burnt them.'

'All of them?'

'All of them.'

'What about your wife's past?'

'I don't know anything about her past.'

'What do you mean? You've been married to her for over a year.'

'Yes. But she never told me anything about it.'

'Previous boyfriends. Anyone who might want to do her harm.'

'I've told you. I don't know anything about her past.'

'She was dumb, wasn't she?'

'Mute. Yes.'

'Any reason for that?'

'Not that I know of. There was no medical reason why she had lost her voice.'

'And now she's lost her body too.' The detective stood up. 'It's a can of bloody worms.'

The detective turned away. 'Looks like I'll be needing *her* soon,' he said sarcastically and pointed to a brightly coloured card that someone had pinned to the wall. It was stuck in the middle of the mosaic of tattered cards advertising small village jobs and lost cats. The card read VENUS DODGE. PSYCHIC DETECTIVE. Her address was somewhere in the city, over fifty miles away. 'I don't know who puts up with these lunatics. Or puts their cards up for that matter.'

He pulled the card from the wall, the drawing-pin landing on the wooden floor with a delicate tinkle, the card also dropping to the floor.

Noah sat for a while on his chair after the detective had left the room. He picked up a copy of *Life* magazine and flicked through the pages. He then put the magazine down on the table and walked up to the door and opened it: it wasn't locked. He peered round into the corridor which was empty except for a poster of a man wanted for a murder in the city, pinned to the faded white walls.

He walked out of the room, closing the door behind him and made his way down the corridor, passing the open police reception on his right. He lifted the latch on the front door and walked out on to the dark street. Judging by the efficiency of these policemen, he thought, he wouldn't be noticed missing for at least another hour.

Noah walked back through the village to his house, checking, before entering the garden, that no one had remained behind to stake it out. The lights of the house were off and the garden was in darkness. He entered the house and ran up the stairs – he knew exactly what he was looking for.

The bedroom had been cordoned off with yellow tape but apart from that nothing seemed to have been moved. The police had not searched the room yet. In the moonlight the bedroom looked eerily beautiful, the blood on the bed like black pools of water. The 'Home Sweet Home' tapestry that Pandora had sewn, with its decoration of small birds and animals playing in each corner still hung on the wall.

Noah got down on his knees in front of the bedroom cupboard and started rummaging amongst the clothes and shoes at the bottom of it. In the cupboard was the only clue he had. But the more he searched the more certain he grew that the box, along with her body, had disappeared.

He heard noises down below in the garden and looked down to see two policemen walking down the path to the front door.

'Murderers are like dogs,' he heard one of them say, 'always sniffing around their own dirt. Always returning to the scene of their crime.

Noah heard them enter the front door which he'd carelessly left open. He ran through to the back spare room, opened the window and climbed out, dropping down to the back garden below. He felt agile, untouched, as if nothing could touch him again. Even the grass that swept his ankles felt new. He ran to the bottom of the garden where he buried himself beneath the bushes and waited, the smell of dark earth around him. It was silent, unjustifiably silent there until he finally fell asleep.

He dreamt of gardens where the flowers and plants were limbs growing out of the soil, the fingers outstretched like the branches of a tree from the trunk of the arm. Skulls formed the backdrop of the hills behind. There was no sense of horror in the dream, just the feeling that the world had irretrievably changed and he now had to accept the new landscape around him.

Noah woke up late the next morning and crawled out from underneath the bushes. He had pushed the image of Pandora into the arena of dreams. Her death had been so shocking it could not really have happened and its horror became his salvation, made it unreal. It became imperative that he left the area, whether in space or memory, where she should have been.

VENUS

'he that increaseth knowledge,
increaseth sorrow'

There was always, in theory, the comforting faded yellow walls of his room, its chipped wooden features and the radiator babbling in tongues. The large square sink in the corner had a black fault running down the white porcelain neck that supported it. The crack changed shape from a bolt of lightning to the delta of the Nile depending on the light. However, the cracks in the ceiling fitted together like the pieces of a completed jigsaw.

There was no room here for disguises. The decoration only added to the room's sense of blankness, emphasised by a single painting of a sailing ship hanging above his bed. Wind billowed out the pale sails of the boat, but the opaque, cobalt sea remained still.

It was a room that many people had lived in, single people at the bluntest point of their lives. The noises in this room always came first, the noises of other people. Noah found it surprising that the reality of other people's lives could trespass into his own so easily, without him having to ask it in first.

He could not make his new location clear to himself nor would he be able to give the details of the room to a stranger. This is where he ran into difficulty. He had always been good at factual descriptions. He had trusted the facts of the empirical world which he had once inhabited with abandon. But now he began to suspect that the place where he lived looked like his new state of mind.

He had moved to the city. Which one he was no longer sure. But he did know he was in an area to the north which everything had abandoned. To the south-west lay the desert. In spite of being in the city, Noah felt sometimes as if he were living in a wild landscape with rough rocky mountains and sandy dunes and the dilapidated buildings around him were only allusions to something else. Yet he definitely heard police sirens at night and their lilac lights would fill up his attic room with their scent. The screams of children in the dark and the sound of breaking glass crystalised his thoughts.

Noah knew that as long as he remained anonymous it would be difficult for the police to trace him. He had drawn his life-savings from a bank on the other side of the city to avoid detection.

He started to roam the streets aimlessly during the day. In his new life he felt oddly free, unconstrained by his previous sense of the structure of time. He had become opportunistic. When he saw an owner leave a house, or a fortuitous piece of scaffolding which he could leap up, swift as a cat, it was the sense of opportunity that possessed him.

He did it for the sound of breaking glass. The catastrophic sound of fragmented glass falling to the ground was music to his ears. Illicit entry was another pleasure. The way a window tried to resist his force, a back-door, the pressure of his arm. He relied on the seizing of a chance: it was not a matter of choice.

In their absence, he wandered round the shadows of other men's homes, picking up objects and turning them over in his warm palm like fetishes. He felt his feet tread on forbidden skin. He turned photographs of daughters and sons to the light. He never stole money but always took away some kind of valueless trinket as a trophy of his undoing.

His attic room gradually became festooned with these odd mementoes: a small china dog, a rabbit's foot keyring, a paperweight with a glass rose trapped inside it, a miniature plastic Eiffel tower. He carefully positioned the objects round the room, at equidistance to each other, on the floor.

He now shared the calm equanimity with which the days were interminably turning into months.

One afternoon Noah looked out of his window and noticed for the first time the house standing opposite. It was symptomatic of his new life to be surprised by the obvious. The white house was large and shabby and detached from tenement blocks on either side. A small patch of garden lay in front, the grass uncut, a bush sprouting out of the ground. A single dead tree grew in the centre of the lawn, its dead silver branches spiking the sky. One of the windows had already been smashed, creating a hole like a black star.

Noah would spend hours staring down at the house, from his seat by the window. He would stay up throughout the night, mesmerised by the light the house shone over the garden. The ground that the light covered looked like a separate world. He felt he could take his time over this house, unaware that, as he waited, time was taking him.

Over the days he noticed that the lights of the house came on at exactly the same time at night, irrespective of the outside natural light, and that the lights switched off at the same time in the morning. He never saw anyone at the windows, nor did he ever see anyone leave or arrive at the front door.

He became convinced that the house was uninhabited. And he began to become obsessed by what the house would look like from the inside, as once he had been fascinated by the internal workings of the body. He wanted to work out what lay inside.

His dreams became fragmented by the sound of breaking glass. The more he waited for the right time, the more his desire to enter the house deepened. At night as Noah slept, the house's light shining through his window from the other side of the road, alleviated the darkness of his room.

One night Noah was sleeping when the sound of hammering at his door woke him up and, flinging on a dressing-gown, he reluctantly opened the door. A little old lady stood in the doorway, her coarse grey hair falling incongruously girlishly in tendrils about her face. Her features were cramped together in the centre of her face, making her forehead and cheekbones loom out, as in a concave mirror. Bare feet peeped out from under her long flannel dressing-gown, displaying painted toenails curved like the beak of a bird.

'Is anything wrong?' she asked. She had the still, deep voice of a man.

Noah could see her peering over his shoulder into his room and noticing the trophies placed like sentinels over his floor. He could see her wondering, and he stepped forward to deliberately block her view. This immediately afforded him the view behind her, over the balcony down the steep drop into the hall below.

The hall sofa had been moved to the centre of the chamber, and Noah could see the indentations that marked the cushions, from where his landlady had just got up. A big second-hand television set stood on the table in front of the sofa, its black and white light flickering over the sofa's faded pink velour. The sound had been turned down.

'Wrong?' he asked, surprised.

On the television screen a tall man in a magician's hat, that reminded him of the policeman who had interrogated him, was solemnly pulling a rabbit out of a hat.

'Yes. I heard screaming from your room,' she hesitated. 'I'm sure it was from your room.'

'When was this?'

'It sounded like the wail of an animal in a trap.'

He tried to work out what she was reading in his face, what conclusions she was drawing, but he couldn't see beyond her curiosity.

She continued, 'As your landlady, I think I have the

right to an answer. As you know, tenants are forbidden to keep pets.'

'I'm sorry,' Noah said, 'I have no idea what you are talking about.'

He quietly shut the door again, removing his dressing-gown and getting back into bed where the damp, nylon sheets stuck to his naked flesh. The portable gas fire was making the room too hot. The gas gave off a sweet heady smell and he went to sleep again to the lullaby of its soft constant hissing, feeling relieved to have reached the end of his previous life to have begun this one.

The next evening he decided to break into the white house. He moved swiftly and silently over the road up the path under the branches of the dead pear tree. He put his hand through the ground-floor window and unlocked its latch. He opened the window and, as he climbed through into the house, he had to pick the shards of glass from his wrist. He was surprised by the newness of the interior: it was all white as if it had recently snowed. He touched the white walls tentatively as if he were expecting the snowflakes to come off on his skin.

All the furniture had been covered in white sheets, material objects looming up in the darkness, their shape and details disguised under a white snowfall. Noah lifted up the white sheets to see what kind of furniture lay underneath but all he could see were objects tightly wrapped up in a plastic which refracted the light and refused to soak in the blood that dripped from his wrist.

The only uncovered object was a large glass cabinet in the middle of the room. Walking up to it he could see that it was filled with the myriad colours of tiny glass animals. Transparent antelopes and elephants were tinted on their ears or tails or eyes, by drops of azure or scarlet, as if touched by a larger hand.

He went up to the bedroom where he looked around for photographs of a family, for scalps that he could carry back to his room. But again the room was empty and white. The only colour in the room leapt out at him: a photograph in a silver frame which was propped up on the mantelpiece directly above the bed.

The man in the photograph was a few years older than Noah. The backdrop was of the plush velvet and odd, hidden lines of a photographer's studio. The light full on his direct gaze made Noah realise why the Indians thought the camera could steal their souls. This man's soul seemed so close to his surface that in the flashlight of the moment it seemed to be being wrenched from its body. Just before Noah was about to slip the photo in his pocket, the gleaming object which the man was holding in his hands caught his attention. It was a glass box, a cube foot, with a butterfly clasp. It was only then that Noah realised with absolute certainty whom he was looking at.

Noah did not remember leaving the white house that evening he just remembered beginning to walk and walk. In theory, he was simply crossing back over the road to his bed-sit – but just not in that direction. He walked until the city opened up and closed in again around him, he walked until the pavement became cracked beneath his feet and stray dogs started to roam the area he had entered, like wolves. An aeroplane flew low over the strange houses' roofs like a piece of geometry cut from the sky.

He walked for hours through the night until dawn brought out the outline of the world again. The photograph in his pocket only reminded him of the sense of loss he had felt since discovering Pandora dead, the loss not only of her but of himself. Months had passed yet he couldn't recover himself, how he had used, in his previous life, to be. He had gone. He had been left with a series of gestures. It wasn't a question of pulling himself together. He had tried and had been left with a cobweb, a cat's cradle, with empty squares between lines of string.

Just as the working day of the next morning was beginning, just as he had managed to fill his head again with the relentless blankness he had become accustomed to (for it requires concentration to forget what he was trying to forget, to assign to oblivion – that kind of forgetfulness is not for the faint-hearted, for the weak), the flashing of a neon light above his head caught his attention. The sign PRIVATE INVESTIGATOR was flickering in livid violet against the side of a dark crumbling building. The s had slipped slightly down like a wayward snake in a game of snakes and ladders. All the letters were slightly wonky, as if the glass had melted from the heat of the neon bulb within. To the right of the sign on the second floor was a window with a cage hanging between the open curtains. Inside the cage a small, yellow bird was swinging from a perch.

When his body turned off the street in the early morning light into the tenement block and up the stairs, it was as if someone else had gained access to his mind. He had not given his written consent. The steep steps were of old stone and curved round and upwards. There was no rail to hang on to and he had to lean, for balance, towards the wall on which large, red arrows, pointing upwards, had been painted at regular intervals.

He knocked on the wooden door at the top. PRIVATE

INVESTIGATOR had been printed on the door's cloudy glass panel. There was no reply but he could see light shining through the opaque glass and the silhouette of a man sitting at a desk, his legs propped up on the table.

As there was no reply, he opened the door on to a large, oval room which surprised him because, from the outside, the walls had been square. The curved walls were lined with old books. Some of their red, leather bindings had crumbling spines. Cobwebs hung from the ceiling. The spaces left between and above the book shelves were covered in prints of maps, but of countries he did not recognise. The room seemed on the verge of collapse, held together by the threads of an arcane knowledge.

The detective was sitting at a desk, in shadows at the far corner of the room, in the process of adding a roof to a house of cards. Noah's walking to the centre of the room did not distract him from his state of concentration.

'Excuse me.'

The detective looked up. He was a lightly built man but Noah was aware that the dexterity of his movements might possess a wiry strength. His still, self-contained expression looked as if his face had been coated in a fine sheen of lava. The centres of his hooded eyes were pinpricked by light, as if an internal light was shining out from them. Noah presumed it was the way the detective was sitting in relation to the morning light that made his eyes shine like that. It was an optical illusion.

Noah took out the photograph he had found in the house and put it on the detective's desk. Noah was careful not to cause a breeze that would knock down his tower of cards.

'I need to find this man.' As Noah said this, he realised how scared he was of the fact that his life up to now had gone terribly wrong, that this was his last chance to get it right.

'What's this in connection with?'

'That's all I can tell you.'

Noah didn't want him finding out the exact details of the case so soon, as he had yet to prove his own innocence. The detective looked at him hard and he saw the detective see something in his eyes. Noah quickly averted his gaze.

'He that increaseth knowledge, increaseth sorrow,' the detective said quietly. He then added 'But I'll see what I can do.'

Noah left the photograph of the man holding Pandora's box, on the desk, his paper face staring up at the ceiling. As Noah walked down the steps, in the opposite direction to the arrows, he remembered he had forgotten to ask the detective his name.

He spent the following week in his bed-sit staring at the picture of the ship. He remained in a state of suspended animation, where the world and he existed, but in a relation that seemed almost pleasantly arbitrary. He could hear the sound of his landlady watching television down below in the hall and the clicking together of knitting needles from next door. He was grateful to the noises, grateful that other people could get on with their lives, that their sounds showed that it was possible to get on with life.

He returned to the investigator's office the next week, considering what it meant to have hope happen to him again. He could feel it begin to trickle down through his mind. As he walked up the steep steps everything seemed as before. The detective's outline was again visible through the glass panel of the door. His silhouette was sitting in exactly the same position. Except this time, when Noah knocked, he said come in.

As Noah walked towards the desk where the detective sat waiting for him, he noticed that the bird in the cage at the window, like the detective, seemed not to have moved. But this time Noah also noticed that the bird's feathers were dried and faded, its body was immobile and its small black glass eyes unseeing. Even the photograph that Noah had left on the desk seemed to be lying in exactly the same position, as if the investigator had not bothered to pick it up. However, in the photograph the expression on the murderer's face appeared more certain.

This time, when Noah approached, the detective stood up with outstretched hand. When he said hello Noah was struck by how quiet his voice was. Noah's imagination could go no further than the detective's voice. Noah had been blinded to his visual past and there was no longer any resonance to anything he saw. He was struck again by how, since Pandora's death, it was as if everything he saw, no matter how many times, was for the first time.

'I'm sorry,' the detective said, 'but I can't help you, after all.'

'You failed to track him down?'

The investigator didn't hesitate. 'Oh I tracked him down. In a manner of speaking.'

The light still shone from his eyes, irrespective of where he was standing in relation to the daylight.

'I'm not interested in fairy stories,' Noah said.

'Perhaps you should be.' Noah was shocked to see a shadow of fear cross the detective's face. 'You would be better to leave this man alone.'

'You've got to tell me what you've found out,' Noah said. It sounded flat but he wondered where he was getting this insistence from.

The detective picked up the photograph and handed it back to him.

'Burn it,' he told Noah.

Noah felt a force that he had never known before. He felt cleansed, washed by his need to find out what the detective had seen that had frightened him into silence. This sense of purpose sensitised Noah to the air around him. The limbo Noah had been living in had vanished. Like a tree that was conspicuous in Noah's barren landscape, the detective now connected the ground to the sky.

Noah would somehow have to find a way of making the detective talk. Noah was impatient with the detective's fear. Noah couldn't guess what the detective had discovered in connection with this man but it could have been no worse than what he himself had seen and now spent his days forgetting. Noah no longer had fear, for he had righteousness on his side. Righteousness was like a black cloak, that flapped about him in the wind like wings, that whipped about his body reminding him again that he was made of flesh and bone.

Noah returned to the detective's office the following

morning but this time when he tried the door the detective had locked it from the inside. Noah could see his figure sitting at the desk in its usual position. Noah shouted through the door, 'I can give you as much money as you want.' There was no reply.

Noah started to stuff banknotes through the letter-box, fifty and a hundred notes. For a while the detective remained sitting, then Noah, with a secret pang of triumph, watched him, through the glass, come towards the door and bend down out of sight to collect the money.

'Take my money,' Noah whispered to himself. 'It's blood money.' But to Noah's shock he saw the money being pushed back through the letter-box, the notes floating slowly down through the air and landing by his feet. The detective put his mouth to the letter-box, and opened it so that Noah could see deep into his narrow throat to the thick root of his tongue.

'I'm not for sale, were the words that came out of it.

Noah had become an expert in stalking the homes and artefacts of other people's lives. Now he began to wait for the detective himself. He watched for him outside his office during the day but whenever the detective saw him he would take evasive action, either crossing to the other side of the road or nipping back into his doorway. Noah went back and back again. He finally cornered the detective in the middle of the road and, as Noah grabbed his arm, cars rushing past them on either side hooting their horns, he was surprised by how fragile the detective's arm felt beneath his jacket.

'You've got to help me. I'll give you anything you want,' Noah said. 'You have no idea how important it is for me to find this man.'

The detective looked at him with a great sadness. 'This man you are looking for. He is not human. He will involve you in great evil. Please believe me. Now leave me alone. If you try and contact me again I will call the police.'

The detective slipped between the cars and was gone. Noah stood in the middle of the road, staring straight ahead and seeing nothing, letting the cars drive round him until night fell.

The next evening Noah observed the office from the doorway of a nearby building, waiting for the detective to leave for home. The lights went off at midnight, but by 12.30 the detective had still not left the front entrance. Noah stayed up all night in vain, waiting for some sight of him. The next morning Noah checked the back of the building but there was no back exit, no fire escape, no back way: the iron spiral staircase was broken half-way down the building and what followed was a forty-foot drop. Somehow, Noah assumed, he must have given him the slip.

Over the next few days, exactly the same thing happened: the lights would go off at midnight but Noah would never see him leave. It was only then that Noah realised what was happening. This wasn't a magical disappearing act. The reason Noah never saw the detective leave was because the detective wasn't leaving. He was staying the night there – his office was his home. When the lights at the window went off, it wasn't the detective leaving, but him going to bed to dream.

Noah now understood what a solitary life the detective led. For Noah had never seen anyone visit him, either during or after work. He had no family and he had no friends.

The next day Noah bought a second-hand car from a nearby garage, choosing the most inconspicuous model he could find. He packed a suitcase and put it in the boot. He then visited a local hardware store and bought a thick rope, coarse and rough that could burn skin easily. He put it in the cupboard next to his bed. Late the same night he drove his car to the detective's street. After the light had gone off in the detective's office, Noah quietly entered the building and crept up the stairs made of a stone so cold he could feel it through the soles of his shoes. When Noah put his fist through the glass of the door, he felt a certain thrill of conviction as he was skilled at doing things in silence.

Walking over to the desk he picked up a glass paper-weight with a butterfly inside it. In a trick of the light the butterfly flickered its wings. He looked around for the investigator and saw him curled up in a ball, his sleeping face turned towards him, in the corner of the room on a mattress, covered by a red, woollen blanket.

Noah brought the paperweight down on the detective's skull, just hard enough to knock him out. The glass met bone with a dull thud and the body relaxed. Noah then pulled back the cover: underneath was the naked body of a woman. The detective was a woman. However, her body was more like an animal's than a woman's — the breasts were barely perceptible, her ribcage as fine and brittle as shell, her limbs twisted in triangles like the legs of a hungry dog. It made no difference to Noah what sex she was.

He wrapped her up again in the blanket and carried her unconscious body down the stairs and along the streets back to his car, passing no one but the odd vagrant sleep-ing in a doorway. Having placed her on the backseat of the car, he drove back to the bed-sit and carried her through the hall and up the stairs. The landlady was too busy watching TV to look up from the screen on which a magician was sawing a woman in half.

He put the detective down on the bed and tied her limbs to the four posts with his rope so she was spread-eagled like a star.

'I need your help,' he said again to her, as she lay unconscious on the bed. He wondered how many times he had now said this to her, on the stairs, from across the road, towards her retreating back, to her profile just before she turned her head, but this time it was more difficult for her to get away.

He looked up at the painting of the ship, that hung above her head, which for no matter how long it sailed, always remained in exactly the same place, and he tried to stay calm. Outside the room he could hear the landlady going upstairs to bed, humming, 'How much is that doggie in the window? The one with the waggly tail.'

He sometimes heard noises outside his room after the bed-sit went black, but saw no light, there was never any light after twelve. It was as if the walls and the roof had disappeared and they were existing under the night sky, as if the structure of the house had collapsed around them both and the Milky Way was staring down.

As Noah looked at the investigator lying on the bed, the

certainty that he needed the detective did not leave him for a moment. He could never track down his wife's murderer on his own. There were not enough clues. The murderer could be anywhere in a country that had lost its fine detail, that was made distinct only by the specific nature of its local crimes.

He covered her with a blanket to keep her warm and waited for her to regain consciousness. As dawn broke, she sat up on the bed, as far as she could, her head peeping over the blanket, like a shrunken head in a museum case.

He said to her quietly, as the stars shone down, 'I'm leaving the city to look for him and I need you to come with me.'

Before she had time to reply, he took a scarf from a drawer, gagged her mouth, untied her, wrapped her up in the blanket again so it covered her face and carried her downstairs out on to the street. He closed the door silently to the hostel with a mixture of relief and regret. He carried her to his car and placed her carefully on the backseat. He was worried by her stillness, and peeped under the blanket to check on her. Her naked body was curled up in a ball as pale and pink as a naked baby rat. He couldn't understand how he had ever been fooled into thinking such a puny body had ever belonged to a man. Her eyes were squeezed tight shut as if somehow that would prevent what was happening to her happen to her.

He knew exactly what he was doing. She would come round to him in the end, once he could tell her what it was all about. It was as if all the bumps and contusions had been flattened out. He had become streamlined. The hope of finding the murderer of his wife had made Noah pure.

Having driven straight through the night out of the city Noah quickly reached the desert, and by late evening of the next day Noah saw lights flickering by the side of the road in the otherwise immense darkness around him. The golden rocks that had studded the plain during the day had disappeared into the shadows.

As Noah drew nearer he could make out the huge neon sign above a low lying building. Flashing in purple were the words LOVE MOTEL adorned on either side by pink hearts pierced by arrows.

Parking the car in the lot, Noah left the detective asleep in the car and walked up to the motel. Even at night, the heat of the desert took his breath away. The motel was in the shape of an E without the central stroke and he entered the motel at the front door where the stroke should have been.

The reception hall was empty. A small cactus stood in a saucer on a high formica desk. A picture of Niagara falls hung high up on the wall – Noah remembered that a tourist had climbed over their protective fence recently, and fallen over them. A little handbell stood on the counter too, next to a sign which read PLEASE RING FOR SERVICE.

Noah was just about to ring it, when a man appeared through an invisible door, below the poster, wearing a cowboy hat. He stood behind the desk and appraised Noah for a moment. His symmetrical face had a blank look, as if it had just been wiped clean but his blue eyes were muddy, as if they had been gratified too often.

'Egyptian. Persian. Or Ancient Greece?' he asked.

'Pardon?'

'The room. Egyptian. Persian. Or Ancient Greece.'

'Er, Ancient Greece, please.'

The man handed him a key with a little, yellow, plastic statue of Socrates dangling from it. The number 7 had been written in indigo felt tip on the front of his toga. The receptionist disappeared through the door again, as if he had never been.

Inside their room, pillars ran along the side in the Corinthian style and the bed's headboard depicted the Parthenon in relief. On either side of the huge double bed, stood life-size, white plastic statues of women wearing togas, each with one breast showing. Through the window, a turquoise swimming pool glimmered in spotlights which had been carefully positioned around its side.

The gagged detective was lying awake on the bed, in one of Noah's T-shirts and a pair of his trousers, her arms tied behind her and her legs tied together. Noah could see that a bruise was coming up on the side of her forehead where he had struck her. She was looking at him almost contemptuously.

'We're going to have to be friends,' Noah announced. 'It's not going to work any other way. I'm going to keep you for as long as it takes for you to co-operate with me. The longer it takes for you to co-operate, the longer you are going to remain my prisoner. It makes sense for *you*, if you help. You know otherwise I am never going to let you go.'

Her apparent calmness disconcerted Noah, as if she could see so far into the future that the present didn't matter to her. She wasn't struggling and didn't seem frightened at all.

That night, Noah dreamt he was asking her where the man was but she was refusing to tell him. He began to shake her violently until her head began to flop forwards and backwards like a rag doll. It suddenly snapped off and trundled across the floor. To his surprise the head then began to speak, uttering the words 'He that increaseth knowledge, increaseth sorrow,' again and again.

The swimming pool was cool blue the next morning and still night-chilled. It was too early to have been cleaned and mosquitoes either floated dead-still on the top, or struggled in the process of drowning. Noah swam for half an hour, quickly and efficiently. He didn't swim for the sensation of defying gravity.

The swimming pool was surrounded by an iron fence and he caught sight of the head of the receptionist walk past him, on the other side of the bars, wearing its cowboy hat. The head gave Noah a knowing smile.

When Noah returned to their room Venus had already woken up; she looked at him with bleary eyes, as if she had grown tired of him a long time ago. He bent over and untied her gag. Noah noticed for the first time the faded tattoos printed across her knuckles: VENUS across her left hand and DODGE across her right. Noah recognised the name from somewhere but wracked his brain in vain.

'Are you mad?' she immediately said. 'Do you think this is the way to get my help? By kidnapping me?'

'It's the only way. The only way out. I have to find this man. Tell me what you know about the man in the photograph and where he lives and I will let you go.'

'I've told you all I know.'

'You must have gone into his background. Found out his history. Met someone who knows him. Or else how did you find out he was evil?'

She shook her head. 'I've only got my visions and dreams.'

'What do you mean, your *visions and dreams*?'

As Noah impatiently spoke, he saw Venus Dodge's card falling, weeks ago, on to the police station's floor. For the first time since he had met the detective, Noah felt despair again.

Noah gagged her as he could not bear to hear any more of her words. Psychic powers ran against all his beliefs as a medical doctor. It was the physical body that he was interested in healing, and the empirical world for which he reserved his respect.

Noah understood clearly that in spite of their spiritual pretensions, it was the occultists, not the scientists, who lacked imagination. The scientists when they discovered a wonder which they could not comprehend would be curious, try to work out the how of it, whereas the occultists, faced with a mystery, would come up with an answer based on preconceptions, which robbed the thing of wonder.

The next day they reached the heart of the desert where endless vistas of golden sand stretched out into liquid gold. The sun was full and pink and low, its rays reaching across the pale blue sky.

Mirages were frequent, blue water stretching out for miles and Noah was convinced every time he saw one that it was real. He couldn't believe that it wasn't. He could see the water shimmering, the red rocks of the desert towering out of the water as it lapped around their edges. He could see the rocks' reflections in the water. He found it strangely exhilarating the way the eye could deceive, the way one could see the world wrong and be absolutely convinced at the same time it was the truth.

Gradually the sun began to turn a deeper red, flooding the whole sky, and casting the low flat plateau in metal shadow. Noah turned to check the expression on Venus's face but she was looking straight ahead.

Having travelled hundreds of miles in a straight line through the desert, they came to a crossroads.

'It's right,' V. Dodge said. 'Turn right.'

It was the first time she had spoken that day. Even stronger than all Noah's ethical and professional beliefs about the occult was the need to find the murderer of his wife, to find out who had killed her and why she had died, and he had no other choice than to suspend his disbelief.

'So you know where we're heading?'

'Oh yes. In the wrong direction. The wrong direction is where you want to go, isn't it? So the wrong direction is where you'll find him.'

Noah was lying on the motel bed, quietly watching Venus sitting cross-legged in front of the TV. She was channel-surfing between wars, fashion shows and *Going for Gold*, and at the same time munching a McDonalds. In spite of her puny body covered by one of his shirts, and her small feet encased in the sneakers he had bought her, her square forehead, determined chin and her blunt fingers all con-figured to make her look like a man. Noah fell asleep trying to work her out.

He woke in the middle of the night to see Venus still sit-ting in front of the TV transfixed to the screen. Transmission had ended on the channel she had been watching and snow had begun falling down the screen. She seemed to be watching something that was happening behind the snow.

Suddenly her arms and legs sprang out like a mechanical toy, as simultaneously her back flung back in a rigid curve. Jerking movements seized her whole body in what seemed to be an epileptic fit. Foam whorled out of her mouth and streamed down over her lips and chin. The foam became pink, as blood from where she had bitten her tongue tainted its spume. While her eyes filled with tears as if her flesh were turning into liquid, her skin glowed red as if being burnt by flames.

In spite of Noah's medical knowledge, he did not move: instinct told him not to interfere with the demons inside her, for these demons were leading him to the murderer of his wife. She slowly began to levitate just a few inches from the floor, jerking like a dervish. Suddenly an invisible force hurled her back down to the ground. She lay there, dead still, heavy as stone.

Words started to come out of her throat, clear and softly as if she were telling a fairy story to a child, in complete contrast to the twisted and guttural position of her body that was lying on the floor.

'Once there was a river of blood which flowed through the desert thick and still-moving. No natural life inhabited the river or lived in its vicinity. The river and the country it flowed through were places of death, the river causing destruction to whatever it touched. One night, limbs, structures, protuberances, began to grow upwards out of this blood. These forms came together in the shape of the body of a woman. Her body had the kind of beauty that is translucent and as she rose up out of the river it was as if she were made of glass. Because she was transparent it looked like the river of blood was flowing through her veins. Only if people dared to walk close up to her could they see she had no face.'

'Pandora?' Noah interrupted before he could stop himself.

Venus did not reply. He got out of bed and knelt down beside her and saw that she had fallen into a deep, almost comatose, sleep. He took a blanket from the bed and covered her with it. Returning to his own bed he spent the night keeping watch over her.

She didn't stir until about eleven the next morning. He watched her rise slowly to her feet and walk stiffly to the door, turning the handle. The door was locked because Noah still didn't altogether trust her. Even though her efforts to open the door were fruitless, instead of returning to bed she remained standing by the door, as if waiting for someone to open it. She turned around, as if to ask for his help, and Noah saw that, although her eyes were open, she was in a sleep-walking trance. Desperate to find out where Venus might lead him now, he quickly dressed and, opening the door for her, followed her outside into the heat.

Venus walked for a mile along the road until she reached a reservation. She walked as if she knew exactly where she was going. Everywhere cacti stood like petrified limbs sticking out of the sand. The landscape around was dry and beautifully static like an image reflected in a mirror. The sand was so hot it burnt Noah's feet, through his shoes, like molten glass.

Noah followed her along a trail, which led off from the main road into the centre of the desert. The trail was marked by bones, pieces of wood and feathers. Venus seemed to be unconsciously following the trail but, as far as he could tell from the back of her short, dark hair, she never looked down, or sideways, but always straight ahead. The trail twisted in and out past huge piles of boulders protruding into the sky, obscuring the direction of the path. Noah felt he was following her into the centre of the hottest place in the world.

They reached a mountain of boulders. To his surprise, Venus started to climb them. She moved with agility, crawling hard-backed and deftly between the crevices like an insect. He watched her disappear over the mountain of boulders that tottered unevenly up into the sky. The sun was beating down, and at the top there was nowhere for her to go but back down, so he decided to wait for her return.

Down below, he found a huge boulder and crouched down within its shadow. He picked up a handful of sand and let the glittering grains slip through his fingers. A scorpion scuttled across the ground, a few inches from his feet. The heat hissed in his ears, but otherwise the silence was as cavernous as the desert.

She had been away for too long now. The sun had moved an inch across the sky. He began to worry: had she fallen and in some way hurt herself? Faint with heat and thirst, he unsteadily stood up and shouted her name. Her name echoed round the silence like a stone falling through water but there was no reply.

Summoning his strength he slowly clambered up the mountain of boulders after her. Each manoeuvre required a concentration of thought the heat seemed bent on pre-venting. On reaching the top the desert stretched out for miles around him, like a golden sea. He was on top of the world, but Venus was nowhere to be seen.

It was then a movement caught his eye far below him on the trail they had taken. A small figure was scuttling back along the trail towards the road. A sensation of panic wrapped him up in what seemed to be someone else's skin. He clambered back down the boulders as fast as he could, and started to run back along the trail. The sun was now burning his face, beginning to transport his thoughts.

At first he thought he had somehow taken a wrong turn, overshot the mark, when the feathers and bones that marked the trail suddenly ran out. He retraced his steps until the trail appeared again. He saw that he had not run off the trail, it was the trail that had run out – or rather, it had been stolen away.

He tried to find traces of their footsteps in the sand, or marks that the bones or wood had left, but the sand was too dry, smooth as silk, to be imprinted. He attempted to head back in the direction of the road using his own judgement but was confronted this time by a sheer rock face. He backtracked and followed what looked like an approximate path in the opposite direction, only to find the same rock face blocking his path.

He realised that the road definitely lay behind the cliff and that he was going round in circles trying to find it. The only way to get to the road was over this sepulchre of rock. Venus would have reached the road by now.

He tried to edge his way up the rock, an inch at a time, before his ankle caught in one of the crevices, twisting badly. He had to climb back down, wincing in pain, his legs and arms covered in the red dust the rock had traced on him. The sun was a pinprick in the sky. He began wandering around the desert again, this time limping, knowing hopelessly that the more he walked the greater the possibility he was becoming increasingly lost.

A lizard flickered over the sand between the towering cacti. The salt in the sweat dripping from his forehead was stinging his eyes. It was then that he saw a pool of water shimmering in a small indentation between two rocks, its glassy surface reflecting back the sky. When he eased himself between the rocks, bending down over the pool to take a drink, he expected to see his face looking back up at him out of the water's reflection. But instead of his face there was only glittering sand, its shards reflecting back the light of the sun.

He lay under an overhang of rock that night, looking up at the stars that pierced the black sky like pieces of broken glass. The moon was a crescent. In the desert he heard only the noise of movements, secret insect lives, the sounds of different textures rubbing up against each other, the sound of frictions.

He was woken up by the sun burning his face. He looked up into white heat. The sun had been killing him softly while he slept. His swollen throat had begun to constrict his breathing and insects were crawling over his skin. They think I've died, he thought, that my body has become a corpse, and he tried to stand up but his legs would not follow the command of his thoughts and he fell back down into the sun.

Having left Noah still waiting for her at the bottom of the mountain of boulders, Venus made it quickly back to the road and ran as fast as she could back to the motel. Searching the room, she discovered the car-keys and his money in a drawer, hidden between the pages of the Gideon bible. She did not care that she had abandoned Noah to almost certain death by stealing away the trail. In fact, trophy-like, the remnants of the trail, its feathers and bones, were strewn across the dashboard of the car, as she drove through the night back towards the city.

She drove through the blackness of the desert following the white, straight ribbon of road that stretched out to the horizon in front of her, congratulating herself on her escape from both Noah and the evil that lay ahead of him. An evil which he had tried to implicate her in.

There was also another fear she had, which Venus could hardly admit to herself. Any form of intimacy with another human being, no matter how slight, was a threat to her gifts of prophecy. It was why, up to the time of meeting Noah, she had led such a life of solitude. She did not want the gift of her visions threatened by anyone, let alone by such an intractable man as Noah.

After hours of driving along the relentless road, she found herself nodding off and she began to pinch her arm hard to keep herself awake. The silence and the darkness around her made her feel as if she were driving through a non-existent place, a place of death. It was then that she realised that someone was now sitting in the car seat beside her: a woman whom she had never seen before, who in spite of the darkness seemed to have an aura of golden light around her. The tenderness of her presence was frightening, as if it represented mortality itself. Her flesh was transparent: skin made of gauze and limbs fashioned from ochre chalk. Her face was like so many paper leaves layered on top of each other, traced by golden thread. In spite of the exquisite features of her face, there was something about her that reminded Venus of the faceless woman in her vision.

'You should go back to him,' the woman said, but the deep voice was that of a man's. 'Otherwise he will die.'

'I don't care if he dies,' Venus said, looking straight ahead again at the stretch of the road illuminated by the car's headlights.

'But aren't you curious as to what will happen if he doesn't? Aren't you curious about his future?'

'I know where his future will lead him. It will lead back to you.'

The woman laughed, a deep knowing laugh.

'It's not for you to protect him from what he wants.'

Noah regained consciousness with the sensation of water being splashed over his face and neck, cool and hard as diamonds. He opened his eyes to see the sun had been blocked out by the face of Venus. She was standing over him pouring water from a plastic container over his head and he opened his mouth and gulped greedily from the falling water. The material world dissolved into the liquid and cold.

Within minutes, for he had been going round in circles, she had led him back to his car, following a trail of stones which she had left behind like the trail in *Hansel and Gretel*.

Noah did not ask Venus why she had returned to him of her own volition, why she had not made good her escape. He thought that by asking, he would sabotage what he thought was the trust she had decided to place, for an unknown reason, in a man who had kidnapped her.

They continued on their journey and as Noah drove, the heat now unnerved him in a way that, before she had abandoned him in the desert, it had not done. Noah had assumed that no one would notice Venus's disappearance for weeks, if at all, as she had led such a life of solitude. But he was still concerned about being traced by the detective from his village, who had interrogated him about Pandora's death. And if by any chance Venus' disappearance did come to light, Noah wondered if the detective might connect him with it.

Noah had always paid in cash in motels but to vary their movements even further they started to sleep in the car, parked by the side of the road. He would stretch out in the front seat, she curled up in the back. They would sneak into motel swimming pools in the morning to wash off the accretions of sweat and grime.

In her underwear, Venus walked hunched along-side the pool, as if by somehow concaving she could conceal the rest of her body. But Noah could quite clearly see her one dimensionality, as if she had pressed her body flat a long time ago between the palms of her hands, which seemed unnaturally large by comparison. Her legs seemed to dangle from their sockets like Pinocchio's. He noticed for the first time that her toenails were painted a surprisingly ladybird red. Again she reminded him of an insect, but this time close up, with its wings cut off. Flesh had no meaning for her, as if it were redundant to the mind. She swam in the swimming pool like the mosquitoes who were trying not to drown.

As Noah drove through the night, listening to the sound of Venus' breathing in the back of the car, he wondered about her sexuality. She had no flesh on her bones, after all. Venus seemed oblivious to the surrounding world, to what she saw, whereas Noah could still remember what the outside world had once been like. Venus' psychic world had no room for the real. She lived in the realm of sound waves and messages from ghosts. Sex is what she could have touched.

Noah was secretly waiting for another premonition from her as they continued on their journey, but he knew that he would have to wait, that it would not be wise to bully the seizure out of her. The visions seemed violent enough without him forcing them upon her, even if he could. He had no idea what substance any future visions would take, whether they would happen in private or in public spaces, whether Venus would be in control of their timing or they would be in control of her.

The next day they stopped at a diner. It was the first time that they had eaten out together in public. Although the early morning light outside was bright, the café's dark furniture and subdued lighting made Noah feel entombed.

The waitress bent over him in a low-cut dress, to pour him coffee, displaying her breasts. She was trying to exert power in the only way she knew how. But Noah was now as pure as the driven snow. The bodies of women were no longer of any interest to him. Since the death of his wife it was impossible for Noah to find another woman physically attractive. He felt it would imply an infidelity which was almost metaphysical, a betrayal of Pandora's very existence. Other women took on a kind of alien quality which kept them at a safe distance. Noah had become a virgin.

'Who was the woman that appeared in my vision. The woman made of glass with the blank face?' Venus asked

'Pandora. My wife,' Noah replied.

'How do you know?'

'Who else could it be?'

Venus had no idea. But his wife's name had struck her. 'Did you know the first mortal woman to be created by the gods was also called Pandora? Forged out of fire and clay by Vulcan, she was sent down by the gods as a punishment to men for stealing their fire. She wasn't altogether mortal actually. She was half mortal and half divine.'

'That's right. Pandora wasn't immortal.'

He looked hard at her face, to make sure that she understood that the Pandora who was his wife was dead, that she no longer existed. He looked so hard at her face it was as if at first he couldn't see it. He was looking straight past it, except a kind of mask, just outside his line of vision, with eyes, a mouth and a nose, was getting in his way. Noisy hands, slight inclinations, as if Venus' whole mind had been bound where once he had just tied her hands. She was interfering with the linearity of his vision.

'I wonder how real your memories of her are?' he heard Venus saying.

'You think I've made her all up? Memories are the only real things I've got left. What's happening to me now is the fantasy. The more specific a thing is now, the more distant from me it becomes.'

He fell silent. He no longer wanted to explain any more. He was fed up with speech. In his heart he had done away with words, words strung together like beads on a thread, with only space in between. Words were no longer necessary – clumsy explanations, manoeuvres, anecdotes. He had found an internal stillness where words had become irrelevant. Why did he need to express himself when he already knew what lay inside his mind?

In their third week on the road Venus had her second fit, and this time the seizure took place in the car as he was driving. It was as if something had taken possession of her, something that had been hovering inside her all the time, and had now slipped out of its box, ripped through her and wracked her in half. She became a double of herself. This double started to emit strange noises, high-pitched, like a rabbit having its throat slit.

Having stopped the car at the side of the road, Noah watched her as she began to shake violently in her car seat: saliva trickled over her lips and her eyes began to roll in their sockets. Her hands started to claw at invisible shapes in the air. She looked monstrous, as those possessed by what is beyond their reason often are.

This time the words came painfully and violently out of her mouth as if she were giving birth to them.

'Everything is in black and white. I see a table marked out by squares. Each square is labelled by a number. On the table lies a disembodied hand of a woman. The fingers, one of them wearing a signet ring emblazoned with a flame, are splayed out as if striking a chord.'

Venus worked to her own rhythm which bore little relation to Noah's world. Even her shyness seemed not to be so much an escape from the outer world as a retreat into the inner. Noah felt no closer to her than on the day he had first met her. She wasn't warm, she wasn't cold. Human characteristics seemed irrelevant to her – she was neither good nor manipulative. Magic and her imagination seemed to be her only sphere of influence.

She herself had been cast under a spell of her own making. A self-bewitchment where people did not figure but dreams and visions and concoctions of words did. The sense of her own power would sometimes occur to her, and Noah would watch her pleasure infuse her expression, actually changing the structure of her face. Venus was about secrets. He had no desire to break into her dreams. For he feared if he did so, it would expose his own dreams too.

They drove through the night. The desert was black – all of a sudden night had fallen like a stone down a well. There was no twilight here, just light, then black. Clear-cut lines. Before they had started their journey everything had been grey. They drove over the desert in the dark.

Suddenly in the basin of desert in front of them lights appeared, shiny like coloured glass. As if some god-child had on a whim bent down over the desert and placed the flashing lights there, like a bright shiny toy in the middle of an empty wooden floor.

'That is where our future lies. Down there in front of us,' Venus said.

LAZARUS

'curiosity killed the cat'

The hotel was large. It was called The Mirage. Its casino lay where its entrails should have been. The eyes of the hotel were rectangular and frequent in straight rows all along its side. Its eyes were always wide open. The hotel was always articulate, like a child constantly greedy for its own satisfaction. It had a wide-open mouth at its front in order to swallow people whole – not only their bodies, but also all the hopes and possibilities attached to them.

To get to their room they had to walk through the casino. They passed scores of video screens which showed the same horse, jumping over the same obstacle, at the same time. Men were positioned behind desks, the same man, watching his stake, in perpetual motion, his face in a constant fluctuation between hope and despair.

Noah was, like these men, addicted to taking risks. Since the murder of his wife, he had become aware of the cruel indifference of life. He wanted to take its indifference into his own hands. The difference between him and these men was that Noah didn't realise he was taking risks, he simply thought he was following a line of thought.

Noah was convinced that this town was the oracle, that it held the promise of the answer to his wife's death somewhere between the neon lights and the clash of money. So he was glad this place that Venus had led him to was so noisy, so graphic, so enticing for it signalled another turning point to his life.

It was a different world, this place, a place of fabrication. It was where people came to change themselves, a place where people could be alchemists, work magic on their lives. Venus slipped into it like a duck into water, for she understood about spells and enchantment.

Noah lay in bed watching the flashing lights light up the room as if they were sleeping in the middle of a fairground. The sky ablazed with fireworks. He listened to the sound of the city's bewitchment of other people and to the air-conditioning hum.

Venus woke him up the next morning and he followed her down to the hotel's subterranean restaurant to drink coffee, thick as tar. Venus looked even more different from other people than she normally did. Her eyes were too big for their sockets like a fruit bat's and her face was drawn up in lines as if by invisible hooks.

'What's wrong?' he asked, not expecting nor wanting a reason for how she was.

'I had another vision. While you were sleeping,' Venus said, matter-of-factly.

'What did you see?' Noah could not prevent the eagerness spilling out over his lips.

'The same woman I saw in my first vision, who was rising out of a river of blood. The woman you thought was Pandora. This time she has a face. A face of perfection.' The face also belonged to the woman who had appeared beside Venus in the car, while she had been driving alone. 'She is floating underwater, downstream, swiftly. This time the water of the river is clear and translucent, but *she* is now made of flesh. Her eyes are open but she is not breathing. She is perfectly still except for her hair which is flowing around her naked body. Her throat has been slit expertly and thinly by a surgeon's knife. The gap in her neck is as bloodless as a fish's gill.'

This vision was even more incomprehensible to Noah than the other two. He had cradled Pandora's dead body in his arms, but he had no memory of seeing her throat cut. In fact, he was sure that it hadn't been. If the visions were not only of the past, but also premonitions of the future, was it possible that Pandora's throat would be slit sometime hereafter? In a perverse kind of necrophiliac ritual? The murderer must have stolen her body for a reason.

And why had Venus seen a surgeon's cut? He hadn't told her he was a doctor. Did she know, by what she was saying, the possible, misguided connections she was making between him and the murderer? How far did her clairvoyancy take her? He had a feeling her powers were confined only to her visions and that, for the moment, he was safe.

A sudden apathy overwhelmed Noah, as if everything was like the desert that surrounded them. The ubiquitous sand, which he could taste, smelling of nothing but dry air covered his thoughts while his body became almost redundant, a vague weight that just stopped him flying into the phantasm of the sky. His personality suddenly had become vulnerable, as if it could now be read like an open book.

At the end of each seating aisle stood a slot machine, positioned confrontationally like a household god. He could hear the sound of past money, turning around inside them, falling into place.

Since arriving at The Mirage Hotel, Venus had begun imperceptibly to change. Her spells had been inside her for so long, that when she now saw them take place outside of herself, in this hallucinatory place, it liberated her.

The exterior and her interior world finally matched. She began to be aware of how her external appearance could cast spells too. The world began to have meaning for her. Noah's cast-off clothes, that she still wore, had begun to reveal her shape. Her flesh had started to show, to swell out, as if her fantasies were blowing her up from the inside.

It wasn't a transformation, it was a metamorphosis. But Noah had never known her anyway, he had only grazed the surface of her. He had no idea what lay inside her head.

A fortnight after their arrival at The Mirage Hotel, five weeks altogether after Noah had kidnapped her, Venus was strolling along the red carpet which enshrouded the floor of the casino. She looked up at the screens which normally showed the horse racing. To her surprise, she saw instead of horses, the images of two people struggling. She could not see the figures clearly as they were in the distance.

Then, suddenly, her own face filled every screen. A man was looming down over her, a knife in his upheld hand. His face was blank. Venus watched in horror from the casino floor, as on film he pierced her eyes with the knife's blade and her blood filled the screen. Screen after screen turned red. Then, as quickly as the images had appeared, they disappeared. As if nothing had happened, horses began to race across the screens again, against the grass-green background of the racing-course. Venus looked anxiously around but no one else seemed to have noticed what she had seen.

She decided to leave the hotel at once. She did not know how literally or figuratively to read this vision – did it mean a loss of her eyesight or of her gift of prophecy, or even of both? But the image was too graphic for her to ignore. She ran up to the room, quickly packed a bag with half of Noah's savings and some left-over food, and took the lift back down to the ground floor. Just then she saw Noah cross the floor on the other side of the casino. She watched his loping intense walk, the way he took up no more or less space than required, his methodical ordinariness, and she also saw crossing with him, walking by his side, the phantom of Pandora. Venus realised that as long as Pandora haunted him, she could not leave him, no matter at what cost to herself.

Venus' visions stopped and there was nothing Noah could do about it. Noah watched in despair as the external world encroached on her internal one, left her nothing to dream with. She had taken on instead the dreams and fantasies of the town, the dreams of the western world. She had lost her gift but she had come out of herself. She had lost the substantiality of her interior world but become braver.

But unlike Noah, Venus realised that there was another reason why she had lost her gift. She had become too close to another human being. She had known the risk she was taking on accompanying Noah, she had always been aware of possibilities, that was how she was. She realised too that they would now only have human ways to find out what had happened to Pandora, that these human ways would have to become extreme.

A few evenings later, Noah was lying on the bed slowly realising that the reality of the city's dreams were becoming too intense for him. In the city, the image of his wife was returning. He attempted to revise her, to make a different sense of her in order to explain her death but he was unable to write her up. Instead he had a variety of images of her superimposed upon each other, a palimpsest. How in the end could he rewrite his wife when the memory of her had now been set as hard as concrete and he could never write a better version?

Noah decided to take a walk outside. Outside of the air-conditioning of the hotel, the air was clammy and cloyed to his skin like wet kisses. The darkness of the evening seemed to exacerbate and exaggerate the heat and sensitise his skin.

He could hear music coming from upstream. He followed its sound to a dilapidated, faded stone colonial building, with KEEP THE FAITH written in pink lettering on a white board hung above a pair of red saloon doors. The saloon doors swung open as Noah followed the music into the cool, hollowed out room, half obscured in darkness.

It was like a cave: the walls were dark and uneven and hewn as if out of rock. In the gloom Noah could make out small, brightly painted statues of the Virgin Mary and Christ on the Cross set into niches around the room. They had tiny electric bulb halos hovering above their heads. Black beards had been painted on to the stone faces of the Virgin Marys and the statues of Christ were wearing various doll-size sequinned dresses. However, blood tears had also been painted on to the Virgin Marys' faces and the stigmata of the Christs were heavily delineated.

There was the faint trace of sweat, a euphoria in the air, and Noah felt a sense of a secret world having been claimed. He could smell the swoon of incense. At first Noah thought the room was empty. Until he noticed someone dancing in a cage, hanging a few feet off the dance floor.

It was his grace Noah noticed first. His lithe and symmetrical body was fluid as if not made of flesh but of liquid that the air made way for. He danced through the words of the music, and between them, and it became difficult for Noah to distinguish between his almost naked body and the melody. He had his head bent, his gaze looking down towards the floor, and it was only when he looked up did Noah recognise him as the man he had come to this city to find.

But as Noah stared, the dancer's face and body seemed to dissolve in front of him and Noah found himself looking no longer at the man who was the murderer of his wife, but at Pandora, dancing in the flickering light of the twisting globe. Her body looked as if butterflies were alighting on it. Her breasts rose and fell with the movement of her arms, the sinuous grace of her body now in the light, while her head hung down so that her golden hair fell over to conceal her face. He had to look away as he remembered how making love to her had been combined with a fear that the act would dissipate her, that they would both break up into tiny pieces.

A strong sensation of absence overcame Noah, a sensation of such acute loneliness that he felt even he himself had become too much to bear. The effect was beyond self-pity, beyond anything except numbness. It was as if he had been hung, drawn and quartered.

When he next looked up there was nothing in the cage except the shadows of swallows flying across its floor. He also saw the man, now fully dressed, walking out through the door. He followed him through the twisted streets, the noise of sirens echoing after him. The man was dressed in inconspicuous clothes and moved swiftly.

Noah knew what he was doing, after waking from his trance, knew that he was walking in the footsteps of the man who held the secret to Pandora's death.

He followed him to a large house surrounded by railings and a security gate in front of it. The tall, white walls of concrete veered off to both sides. A security camera was positioned on each corner of the gate, looking down at him with its flickering red eye. Written on the gate in gold lettering in immaculate font was DO NOT BE AFRAID OF WHAT YOU WANT. It was impossible for Noah to see over the wall, impossible for him to bear witness to what was inside.

That same night, at exactly the same time as Noah had seen the vision of Pandora dancing in the cage, Venus first caught sight of the hand she had seen in her vision. It was a distinct hand, moulded more like a woman's than a man's, tapered at the fingers and wearing a signet ring emblazoned by a flame. It was lying on the numbered squares of a casino board. In real life however, the hand was not disembodied. The hand belonged to the man they had come to this city to find.

There was a strange aura about him. Venus saw auras around only those people with an intensity of both emotion and consciousness: auras did not distinguish between these two qualities. White interference fell over Noah; the whiteness of landscape hemmed in by snow, but also the whiteness of static, noise. But this man was enclosed in black space. This did not frighten her because of black's common connotations of evil but because of the true nature of black: the absence of colour. She had never seen someone with an aura that negated itself before.

She watched him gamble for a while. Everything he touched seemed to turn to gold, whichever number he chose. The croupier who turned the wheel did not blink, as if the man wielded some kind of power over everyone he came into contact with, as if his expectation that Fortune was on his side, forced those in his vicinity to accept this also. Not even curious about his increasing success, the other gamblers drifted off and left him alone to amass his winnings.

Venus, struck by his aura, could not remember afterwards how he was dressed. The only physical detail she could remember, apart from his hand, was the face that matched the photograph completely. She could only see in him what she recognised, what she had seen before. It was only his aura that she could see for the first time.

Venus rushed in breathless to their bedroom where Noah was lying on his bed, as if he had never got up, as if he were in exactly the same position as where she had left him lying.

'We've come to the right place,' she said. 'I've seen him.'

'Who?'

'The man in the photo. Who do you think?'

The brown and beiges of the room suddenly transformed into bright yellows and greens. The walls turned to glass through which the dreams of the city glared. He suddenly felt his body land on the bed, as if before it had been airborne just above the covers, in contact with nothing. It was only then he had realised that up to this point he had been hovering.

'What does he look like?'

'Just like his photograph of course. The spitting image. Just as he appears. Did you expect something different?'

'Not really.'

She laughed. 'Just in your head then.'

Noah did not reply nor tell her he had seen him too, at the same time as she had spotted him. Her face looked eager, as if the sighting of him had in some way changed her. She was shedding the dreams of the city that had come up to replace her own. This man would take the place of all their dreams, answer them back, but they were still not under his spell. They were preparing themselves for this, without knowing what they were doing.

'You'll have to tell me now,' Venus said. 'Why you are looking for him? Is he in some way connected to your wife's death?'

'She was murdered. And I believe that this is the man who killed her. Then stole her body.'

'What proof do you have?'

He wondered if anything could surprise Venus for she hadn't batted an eyelid.

'There are three things that connect him to Pandora. Firstly, a case of glass animals that I noticed in his house, back in the city. Secondly, a glass box of Pandora's that was stolen from our bedroom after she was killed. Do you remember the photo I showed you of him? It had him holding it in his hands. And thirdly, some letters. Before she was murdered she kept on receiving letters saying DO NOT BE AFRAID OF WHAT YOU WANT. He has those words on his gate.'

'But do you have proof that he actually killed her? You haven't even got a body to show that she died.'

'Who else could it be? Pandora had no family, no history, she hardly left the house. It has to be the person who wrote the letters. The timing between the letters and the murder is too much of a coincidence.'

'But why did he murder her? Was he having an affair with her?'

Noah could hardly believe he was able to respond so coolly. 'I don't see how. When. There were no clues. Towards the end she was cracking up, not acting like a woman in the throes of a passionate love affair. No, I know this man is the murderer of my wife. What I don't know is his connection with her and why he killed her. That is what I have come to this town to find out.'

Noah decided to return to KEEP THE FAITH. It was late at night and this time the bar was teeming with people – loud music thumped through the room and now dancing girls gyrated in the cage wearing nothing but loin cloths. There was no sign of the man anywhere.

At first Noah thought that there were both men and women in the bar but when he looked more closely saw that the men were actually women dressed up as men. The women were playing butch or effeminate, either with cropped hair and tattoos or in Armani suits. There were transexuals as well as transvestites. And then Noah realised that some of the women were actually men. A woman with perfect breasts in a bikini top dancing in one of the cages had the traces of a beard shadowing her chin.

Noah approached a woman standing behind the bar whose pale face was made paler by the thick, dark hair that swept down over her cheek. Noah noticed that beneath her tight, black dress her breasts were perfectly round and full. Her petulant, sensual, scarlet mouth dominated her face, as if it had been let loose to play havoc with her future. She was wearing round her neck a golden pendulum inscribed with the name DELILAH. Noah showed her the photograph.

'Oh. That's Lazarus, the sculptor. He's always here,' she said with a slight lisp. 'He has an insatiable appetite for pretty women. If you know what I mean.' She looked Noah up and down. 'But you're a real aren't you? A real man. I would keep away from him if I were you. He doesn't like real men. They get on his nerves.'

When Noah returned to the hotel room, Venus was sitting on the bed watching an old American comedy film and laughing. It was the first time Noah had heard her laugh, it was a strange laugh, more like someone crying than laughing. For the first time since Pandora's murder he felt touched by an emotion that brushed his cheek like a bird's wing. With that gentleness came a kind of desire.

He sat down beside her on the bed. She seemed oblivious to his proximity but he knew that she was aware of him sitting next to her. He could see the soft down on the nape of her neck. He remembered reading that, according to an ancient religion, if you blew on the back of someone's neck you could possess them.

'You're a real, aren't you?' he asked. They both still had their faces turned towards the screen in front of them.

'A real what?'

'Woman.'

Venus laughed. 'Sometimes I'm not so sure. What does being a woman mean?'

She had turned her head to look at him and they were only inches away from each other's mouths. He lowered his eyes.

He was unable to kiss her. He was impotent.

'You know I can't. Not until I can put her body to rest. She still haunts me.'

'I know that,' Venus said. 'But by then it will be too late.'

Noah spent the time watching Lazarus's house, as he had once watched what he now knew to be his other house back in the city. He knew that in spite of his driving through the desert he had come full circle, was following a recurring theme he could not get out of his head. Noah watched as Lazarus came and went at all times of the day and night, bringing back women to his house. Women who were highly made-up, wearing clothes that stuck to their bodies, and heels that kept them on their toes. Noah watched how he always came out again alone.

Noah wanted to get close to Lazarus, to get inside his mind but he didn't want to risk Lazarus guessing who he was, otherwise he would find out nothing. He decided he would have to make Venus the bait. She would find out the information for him.

Noah dressed Venus up in the trappings of desire. Venus had already lost many of her inhibitions, so without a murmur she flouted her small breasts even more, pouted, flicked her hair, and painted her lips sticky plum. Noah dressed her the way the women Lazarus chose always dressed.

'You have to make him want you,' he said.

Venus nodded.

Every night she strolled through the casino, dressed up to such a point of femininity that her boyish figure looked as if it were in drag, trying to catch sight of Lazarus in vain.

Every night she would return to the hotel bedroom where Noah would be waiting expectantly for her for news. Undressing, her clothes had been wrapped so tightly round her that they left their marks on her skin.

On the third evening, and a month after they had first arrived at the hotel, she walked into the casino and saw Lazarus at one of the corner tables playing roulette. Lazarus looked up at her as she sat down, as she was now difficult to ignore. 'I've seen you before,' Lazarus said to her. 'At the casino. You look different now.'

Over the next couple of nights they met at the same table, but each time, as he got up to leave, he made no attempt either to make conversation or take her home with him. He simply nodded his head. It seemed that his weakness for young women did not extend to her, no matter how available she made herself to him.

Venus had started to notice how soft his voice was, how soft his skin was. Her sensory perception had become alert. The world had turned into colour overnight, her life had become a celebration. Even his suit was of soft fabric, he looked liquid. His obvious beauty seemed to merge into his surroundings, as if by dint of sheer will power he could choose to be inconspicuous. She wondered how such beauty could be so evasive. But it was. As if he were always just giving an impression of himself and the mould was locked away somewhere in a soft, safe place.

On the seventh night, she knew as soon as she saw Lazarus that this time it would be different. He had a distracted look in his eyes, as if he were seeing into the future. At the same time, when he did look at her, he was more attentive, as if to compensate for his otherworldliness. She realised then, that she had very little control over what his intentions were.

This night, as he stood up to leave the gambling table, he stretched out his hand to her. Venus took it. With her other hand she bent down to pick up her coat from her chair. As she did so, her back was momentarily turned to him. She felt a slight breeze on the nape of her neck, as if someone was gently blowing on the skin there.

A car arrived to drive them to his house, the gates invisibly opened and she watched the red light of the security cameras flicker. She felt the burden of Noah's desires to find out upon her – the emphasis of his wishes had been transferred on to her.

They drove into a huge courtyard. Here it was so quiet and secluded that it felt like an oasis or a mirage, an atmosphere both transparent and full of instability. The turquoise light of the flame-shaped swimming pool flickered over the bone white bodies of the naked male and female statues that lined its sides. A brightly coloured mosiac, which depicted Athene coming out of Zeus' head, had been cut into the bottom of the pool. The image was fluctuating under the water with the breeze.

But it was the giant building that stood at the back of the courtyard that disconcerted and intrigued Venus the most. It was not so much a house as a palace. The structure reached up into the sky, a series of arches like the huge nave of a Norman church, each arch slightly higher than the last, until the final one almost seemed to touch the sky. The roof fluctuated over the arches like an accumulating wave. It seemed to be made of brittle glass, but it looked as if it was made of water.

As they drew nearer Venus realised it was not made of glass, but of mirror, and the whole external world was reflected in it. The palace reflected the person who looked at it back, gave nothing of itself away. It was made up of everything but itself.

Venus watched herself and Lazarus approach in their reflections. She was struck by how unrecognisable she was, how much she had changed from her previous self. She felt her new distorted image represented her no more or less accurately than before. A translation always took place between inside and outside. She could never be convincing as an object of desire, there were traces of her visions still hovering around her causing too much static.

She looked at Lazarus and saw, understood, that he had not been taken in for a moment by her trappings, that actually he might be wanting her for something else altogether.

She hesitated just outside the mirrored door.

'There's no need to be frightened,' he said, half-laughing at her, flirtatiously.

She looked up at his reflection in the wall of the palace, but reflected in the mirror was a look in his face that was now acutely focused on the present. The contradictory emotions she had noticed in him earlier in the evening had dissipated into the night air.

'I'm not frightened,' she said, following him inside.

Noah waited for Venus to return. A day and a night passed but it became apparent to him very soon, crystal clear, that she had disappeared. It was as if he had sent a satellite into space and only the stars were now visible. He felt all the anger that a scientist would if the information he had sent the satellite out for had failed to materialise. There had been an act of sabotage. The search for the murderer of his wife, and her dead body, filled up all his emotional and intellectual space, in spite of the gentleness he had momentarily felt for Venus. It was as if his insides had had molten gold poured into them, which had then hardened.

He watched the house fearing the worst as, after the disappearance of his wife, he took the worst for granted. That Venus had gone didn't seem incongruous. Neither she nor Lazarus came out from behind the walls he had never seen over.

He took to playing the casino in The Mirage to bide his time, and over the days won as much as he lost, maintained an equilibrium. Two weeks after she had disappeared, Noah looked up from the turning wheel after an unexpected winning streak, to see Venus sitting opposite him.

He didn't recognise her at first. Gone was her femininity in drag to be replaced by a different kind of disguise, the disguise of money. She was wearing a diamond studded dress and diamond earrings and this time her face was perfectly painted over. *What had Lazarus done to her?* The sequins of her glass-white dress refracted the lights of the casino so she seemed more light than human. Any defects of human nature had been erased. Venus' power of enchantment had turned to herself – she had cast a spell of beauty over herself. She looked like an immaculate version of femininity.

'Venus,' he said as if the name would somehow bring her back to him. She looked at him and he was not prepared for the look of hatred in her eyes, it caused a sharp pain to his heart.

'It's Noah,' he said, astonished. 'Noah. I didn't know what had happened to you. I thought something terrible might have happened.'

But he was more interested in Pandora and before he could help himself, he asked 'What have you found out about her?' while the croupier silently turned the wheel.

'Leave me alone,' she said. 'It's you I've found out about. Lazarus has told me everything.'

As she stood up and walked away from the table, he noticed that she was wearing glass shoes. The wheel was still spinning as he listened to the click of the silver ball fall into place.

Running after her, he caught up with her at the entrance and grabbed her by the hand but the diamonds on her fingers scratched his skin. She seemed to exude some new power, a force external to her that was being channelled through her.

It made him uneasy as he could no longer treat her in the same way. He no longer felt he could trust her, she was like a different person, as if she had been replaced by a double. But this double couldn't trick him. He knew that it wasn't the real Venus. It was an imposter who just looked like her. And he was still only just at the beginning.

'He's bewitched you,' Noah said.

Venus turned her smooth face to him. Her hair was pulled back from her face stretching her skin taut, as if she were walking into the wind.

'No,' she said. 'He's just told me the truth.' Her eyes were opaque, he could see no whites, just crocodile eyes.

'And what's the truth?' But as he asked, he suddenly realised that he didn't want the answer, not now, not at this time. Before she could reply he had walked past her into the night where the palm trees were blowing.

Noah had lost Venus. Whatever lies Lazarus had plied her with, whatever enchantment Lazarus had cast over her, Noah knew that Lazarus had exploited certain vulnerabilities which the loss of her gift had opened up in her. Just as the susceptibility of her nature had taken on the dreams of Las Vegas, so now she had taken on the fantasies of Lazarus. He could only guess what Lazarus had said about him to her, but he knew that her ability to believe in these stories had not so much to do with disloyalty as to do with her fragility.

He did not feel betrayed – after all, the only person who had it in her power to betray him was Pandora. But he felt saddened by what had happened to Venus, unhappy that she had fallen under this murderer's spell. Now, combined with his need to find out why Lazarus had killed Pandora, was his feeling that he must rescue Venus from this man's hold over her.

Due to Noah's single-mindedness in finding out the evil done to his wife, it did not occur to him that Venus was in actual danger, for hadn't already all the damage that could have been done, been done to Pandora?

The next evening Noah lay in wait outside Lazarus's gates until he saw Venus come out with Lazarus, saw the red light of the security camera flicker. As they exited, Noah slipped through the closing gates into the courtyard where the swimming pool was shimmering. The lights of the town were reflected in the mirrored walls of the palace. He pressed on the door that reflected him back and it opened silently replacing his face with the darkness inside.

In spite of the blackness Noah knew immediately the space around him was cavernous. He switched on the lamp beside him: the stem was made of bone in the shape of a woman's torso.

*

He was in the middle of a room of sculptures all carved out of bone. The bone sculptures were beautiful, so polished that they looked wet, dipped in dew. The stalactites of bone hung over in various shapes, seeming to weep into patterns that the sculptor had made. Lazarus could make the bone curve like a pitcher with a ball or come straight to a point. They were like stalactites in fineness or thick as tree stumps. It was as if Lazarus had been drawing in thin air. The bone followed like a pen what his eyes had seen. Intricate patterns like snowflakes hung from the ceiling and hands protruded from the walls. Limbs came out of the floor. There was no flesh in the room. The mirrored walls inside reflected glass and bone. There was a glass cupola above through which the stars shone down.

At night the sculptures seemed to shine like moonlight, like pieces of moon, the shadows of night showing up the exquisite indentations. They were so fluid, they seemed almost to move. Noah caressed them like fetishes, ran his fingers along their edges, his lips, tense, following their line. His eyes concentrated both on their curves and the sensation of touch, their brittle, fluid form. He suddenly felt scared. Scared of the power of their form, and the plea- sure he was taking in them. Pleasure still seemed strange to him.

He felt the bones inside him break in half, splinter, cut

into his flesh. Like shards of glass travelling through his bloodstream straight into his heart.

At the centre of the palace was another smaller courtyard which he entered through a door in the mirrored walls; feeling as if he were going into box within box. A fountain splashed in the middle of the courtyard. Standing in the centre of the fountain on a marble plinth, in the midst of its spray, was the stone statue of the goddess Pandora. A singing ringing tree rustled silver in the breeze, overhanging the statue and casting shadows over it. Noah was struck by the resemblance the statue had to his dead wife.

Her head was slightly inclined to the left, as if listening to the sound of the water. For the first time Noah became aware of the sound of trickling water in the dry city. The fountain's running water had been always there, now he came to think of it, inescapable, since he had first entered the outer courtyard of Lazarus's palace.

In her hands, the statue of Pandora held an opaque glass box. The box had a criss-cross of iron bars webbing it, and a butterfly clasp for a lock.

The sound of human voices mingled with the water of the fountain. Lazarus and Venus were returning. There was nowhere to hide in the small inner courtyard so Noah ran back into the main room and crouched down behind one of the sculptures of a giant hand. Its fingers blocked out his reflection.

He heard them walk into the room and their voices stop. He thought at first they had become aware of someone else in the room, until he heard the sound of sequins and glass hitting the floor. In the mirror's reflection behind them, Noah saw that Venus was now standing naked in front of the still fully clothed Lazarus. Lazarus was feeling her body slowly and languorously as a blind man might have felt a sculpture, his hands tracing the outline of her flesh.

Lazarus then bent down to pick up her dress and handed it over to her.

'Why do you stop?' she asked.

'Because I am only interested in what I can see.'

As Noah watched Venus dress, he could only think to himself, he has done this before, he must have done this before. With Pandora.

In the shadows of the singing ringing tree Noah was waiting for Venus. He grabbed her arm in a vicelike grip and hissed in her ear, 'What has Lazarus said about me? What did you mean when you said you had found out all about me? That you had found out the truth? Can't you see he's telling you *lies*. To protect himself. He's told you it was me who murdered Pandora. Hasn't he? That's what he's said. Are you *blind*, Venus? Do you really think I could have done something like that? Murdered my own wife? Cut off her breasts? *Mutilated her?*'

Venus couldn't look at him straight in the face. But her voice was calm. 'Look into your heart, Noah. Is it so impossible? Can you tell me exactly what happened that night? You can't remember can you? Why do you think that is?'

And Noah couldn't remember all the details of that night, no matter how hard he tried. He just remembered waking up in the middle of the night, turning to her, and cradling her dead body in his arms.

'Is it not possible that somewhere in the recesses of your mind lies the answer?' Venus said quietly. 'Give up, Noah. For your own sake. Let Pandora rest in peace. Leave her be.'

But who was Lazarus? *Where did he come from*? Noah could find no history of him when he checked up the records. He had no birth certificate, no insurance number, no bank account. According to the records the palace was an empty parking lot. As far as society was concerned he did not exist.

In desperation he returned to the night-club to see if he could find some information about him there. Delilah was still standing behind the bar.

'Still hot on his heels are you?' she asked. 'A cuck-olded husband perhaps, wanting his revenge. You'd be surprised at the number of strange men we get in here looking for Lazarus. With that same haunted look in their eyes. You never get women looking for him though. They must always get what they want first time.'

She laughed, revealing a row of perfectly white teeth and then seemed to take pity on Noah.

'Look. I've got something back home that might help you understand Lazarus, just that little bit more. The bar is going to close in an hour if you can wait until then.'

In the early hours of the morning she led him through back streets, through the shadows, to a huge warehouse where they took a freight lift up to the top floor, the spaces between its metal ironwork revealing the crumbling plaster of the building's walls. Her door was made of metal and covered in unintelligible hieroglyphics.

He followed her into a wide, dark room with large swathes of black velvet hanging above their heads making the ceiling artificially low. From the rich, thick fabric hung shining amulets, glass chimes and crystals. The walls were painted a lush purple, covered in what looked like mirror writing. A strong smell of incense was rising up from the blood-red carpet. A row of plastic skulls, lit up by candles from the inside, sat on the gothic mantelpiece grinning at him. Piles of astrology books sat high up on the desk.

Noah suddenly realised the gulf between Venus' type of divination and these fetishes and artefacts on show in front of him. This sorcery was of a different kind of magic to Venus'.

Up to this point Noah had been forced to accept Venus' help as a means of tracking down Lazarus. He had also been forced to accept that her magic worked. But he had neither forgiven himself nor her for the intellectual dubiety of this fact. However, surrounded by such hocus-pocus, he was beginning to see Venus' visions in a different light, to see them simply as the extreme point of her imagination.

'Do you really need to believe in something this much?' he asked Delilah, but she had already disappeared into the kitchen and a few minutes later came out bearing a drink. As she handed it to him, Noah caught the smell of something noxious and politely declined.

'You must drink it if you want to find out about Lazarus,' she said. Noah reluctantly swallowed it in a single gulp, trying not to think what permanent damage the potion might do his synapses.

The drink immediately plunged him into an ecstatic present. Simultaneously, anxieties about the past disappeared down a thin, white tunnel. He sat on the chair, paralysed, unable to move as Delilah bent down over the chair and put her lips to his. He at first thought, in a bizarre moment, she was trying to suck his life from him, that she had become his Nemesis.

'No,' he murmured. 'No, I can't do this,' as she pulled him to his feet and led him unsteadily to her bed.

'Yes you can,' she said as she undressed him and they both climbed between the sheets. It was only as she began to make love to him that it dawned on Noah's hallucinatory state that she had no breasts, that her shoulders were broad and strong and her arms were thick with muscles. He could feel a warm hardening penis between his legs that was not his own. She had been transformed into a man and by that time it was too late for him to want to say no.

He woke up the next morning back in his hotel bed, fully dressed with a splitting headache, unsure whether what had happened had been a delusion or a reality. The point was that he seemed no nearer to finding out about Lazarus – Lazarus seemed to have no past, no history, and the people who surrounded him led fabricated lives and spoke in code.

Now that Venus was no longer on his side, Noah decided he would have to meet Lazarus himself. Noah was prepared to take the gamble that Lazarus wouldn't recognise him. Although Lazarus may have lied about someone called Noah Close to Venus, Lazarus still wouldn't necessarily know what Noah Close looked like. As far as Lazarus was concerned, Noah was still only a name.

Returning to the night-club, Noah decided to take a short cut down the dark streets that ran behind it. A pubescent boy, standing at the top of the street, offered him a broad-sheet which listed the town's nearest live-shows. Noah let it drop down into the gutter.

Turning right at the bottom of the street, Noah became aware of footsteps behind him. He guessed they belonged to someone with a long stride and a light build, as the steps were one for every two of his and padded softly. As Noah walked faster down the street so did the footsteps following him.

Noah pretended to stop abruptly at something that had caught his eye in a shop window. He saw, reflected in the glass, a tall, thin man watching him, dead still, from the other side of the street. He wore a heavy, dark overcoat and his face was in shadow.

Noah continued on his journey, trying to repress an ever increasing sense of panic and turned sharply to the left. The footsteps still sounded behind him. Anything outside his single-handed hunt of Lazarus, Noah could not handle. The idea that someone was now following him was unbearable.

Noah quickly nipped into the doorway of a shop and crouched down within its shadows. He watched with relief the man walk hurriedly straight past him, his face still hidden. Noah waited until the echos of the man's footsteps had disappeared down the street.

Noah arrived at the night-club ten minutes later, out of breath, but relieved to have shaken his pursuer off the scent. Delilah gave him a smile from behind the bar that reminded him of the enigmatic smile on the statue of Pandora's face. Noah sat down on one of the stools, ordered a drink and waited for a sighting of Lazarus.

At eleven, Noah looked up at the cage to see Lazarus dancing in it. Noah became seduced again by his dancing and wondered if this is how the gods had once danced to entrance the mortals.

Towards midnight, Lazarus approached the bar where Noah was sitting and Delilah turned to Lazarus and said, pointing to Noah, 'Someone is looking for you.'

Whatever else Lazarus did, Noah thought, he inspired loyalty.

Lazarus turned, saw him and smiled. Then slowly he walked over to him. In spite of his litheness he had a heavy build. His dark ambiguous expression was magnetic, he drew the gaze to him. The flatness of his face gave more blunt force to a hidden will. In Lazarus's ambiguity lay his power. He created instability in the viewer, in how he should be perceived, and just by looking at him, Noah suffered vertigo. Lazarus sat down at the bar next to him.

'You know what makes people powerful? What makes me strong?' Lazarus's slurred words made him sound slightly drunk. It was only after he had met him a few times that Noah realised this was just the way he spoke.

Noah shook his head.

'A lack of imagination,' Lazarus continued. 'Imagination is a dangerous thing, you know. It makes you weak. Makes you susceptible.'

He then laughed. A languorous look came over Lazarus's face, as if he had only just woken up to the world. But he did not seem to be remotely curious as to why Noah had been looking for him. He swallowed his drink in one gulp. One minute Lazarus seemed to be in one place and the next walking out of the door. Noah never doubted Lazarus's ability to be in two places at the same time.

Every night Noah would return to the bar, quietly

observing the dancers and the cross-dressers, for watching was what he was good at. Noah still thought that watching offered some kind of protection, meant that he couldn't get involved to the point where it would count.

Noah observed Lazarus talking to strange women, to friends who frequented the bar, and was disturbed to see how Lazarus seemed to take on the face and the expression of the person he was talking to, reflecting back the person he was with to themself, like a mirror. But the person did not seem to notice, only becoming more animated and captivated by Lazarus, the more Lazarus looked like him.

Certainly when Noah exchanged a word or two with Lazarus, he wondered if someone watching them talk would notice the same thing happening – that Lazarus would be taking on Noah's face, without Noah realising it. Even with the most *femme* of *femme*s Lazarus took on their features and expressions, giving back to them their hidden, voluptuous glances. Noah realised that this was an important facet to Lazarus's power over people, his ability to give them back themselves, give back their faces, and reflect back their otherness.

A week after Noah's first meeting with him, Noah entered the club to see Lazarus sitting at the bar where he himself normally sat, reading a book. The cover of the book was of an X-ray image of a man and woman holding hands. It was a book on medical surgery. Noah, without saying anything, bought himself a drink and sat down next to him.

Lazarus looked up at him: 'The miracles of modern science. It is amazing what they can do to a body burnt beyond recognition. It's an act of creation in itself. Like the gods. I wonder what it must be like for the patient. To be fashioned like that. To be defined so irrevocably.'

Noah didn't reply. What kind of game was Lazarus playing with him?

'But I've seen you sitting in the bar nearly every night,' Lazarus continued. 'Just watching. What brings you here?'

'I like to watch you dance.'

'But you're a married man.' Lazarus pointed to the wedding ring that Noah still wore.

'My wife is dead.'

'I'm sorry. So now you're interested in men?'

'Not just any man. You.'

'I shouldn't raise your hopes.'

'I'm not interested in you for that reason.' Noah couldn't stop giving himself away.

'Oh. Then for what reason?'

'I'm interested in your connection with my late wife. Have you ever known a woman called Pandora?' Noah wanted to bite off his tongue for giving the game away so early. He also wanted to continue asking Lazarus questions for ever.

'So you must be Noah. Dr Noah Close. What a wonderful name. Like a shut-in flood. Yes. Venus has told me all about you.'

'And you have told her all about me.'

'Only what I read in the papers. The husband caught literally red-handed. His escape from custody. You must be nervous. It's wise of you to avoid the police.'

'So you've been following the case.'

'I'm always interested in a good murder.'

'Why did you do it, Lazarus?'

Lazarus didn't miss a beat. 'You mean murder your wife? You think I am a murderer because of a series of coincidences involving glass boxes and letters? Why should I know anything about the death of your wife? Why don't you just face up to your own guilt instead? The whole world knows it.'

Lazarus laughed. His eyes reflected back light.

'Don't think you can work spells on me,' Noah told him 'I'm not susceptible to your suggestions. I'm not subject to enchantment. Unlike Venus, I have no imagination. I only have the fact of Pandora's death. And the knowledge of my innocence.'

'But you don't, do you, Noah? You don't have the knowledge of your innocence. And without your imagination you will never find out anything. Or anything worth knowing.'

Noah reached out across the space that separated them and put his hands around Lazarus's neck. Everything about Lazarus was deliberate, worked out. Noah felt that all those who came into contact with him had already been worked out by him, their actions would always fail to surprise him.

Lazarus laughed.

'Physical acts are so easy, believe me. But it would be a mistake. You would never find out what happened to Pandora. The unanswered fact would stick like a craw in your throat for the rest of your life. Besides, you're in a public place. Normal people would stop you.'

Noah withdrew his hands. He had been surprised at how soft Lazarus's neck had been – he had thought it would have been sharp-edged like glass, but the flesh sunk in beneath his fingers like clay.

'So you admit that you know her? That you can give me an answer.'

'What does knowing someone mean?' Noah noticed that the indentations of his fingers still marked Lazarus's neck. 'Sometimes I feel I haven't met you at all, Dr Close.

Just as I'm getting to know you, you say something, do something, look in a certain way, that turns you into a phantom or ghost. Suddenly you don't seem quite real. If one looks in a certain way at anyone, one can turn them into strangers. I like that. The sacredness of the individual. How can you ever dare to know someone intimately, *really*. How can you hardly dare to know *yourself*? Most people are strangers to themselves. Going around with a stranger living inside their head. Like a parasite, doing unpredictable things, surprising them, often far ahead of their intentions. How terrible it would be to understand that stranger inside. To actually get to know oneself absolutely. Suddenly to think to oneself "I *know* you. You'll never surprise me again."'

'You haven't answered my question.'

'I'm sorry, I thought I had.'

'I'm going to find out, you know,' Noah said. 'Find ou the truth.'

'Of course you are,' Lazarus replied.

NOAH

'to feel like oneself again, to
feel risen from the dead'

With a heavy heart, Noah walked down the dark narrow streets back to the hotel. It took him a while to realise that the same light, long footsteps that had been following him before had started up again, behind him. Instinctively, Noah started to run. Then the footsteps matched his speed. They began to gain on him and after a few minutes, pale and exhausted, Noah decided to give up trying to run. He wanted to let the truth catch up with him, instead of the other way round. Coming to a stand-still, he turned to face the man who had been pursuing him.

The man towered above him, his features obscured in the darkness of the street.

'You're a messenger,' Noah said, looking up at him, half eagerly, half fearfully. 'Have you been sent by Lazarus?'

The man stood on the narrow pavement as still as the shadow of death.

'In a manner of speaking,' he replied.

The man then deliberately turned his face up to the light of the half-moon so that Noah could recognise him. It was the same detective, from his home village, who had interviewed Noah in the aftermath of Pandora's death.

'We've been looking for you, Dr Close. For a long time.'

Noah was surprised by how little the detective's face had changed, feeling irrationally that the detective's face should have reflected the changes that had happened to him since being on the run. But on reflection Noah realised that the detective had been resolute in his hunt for him so why should his face have changed when nothing else had? He had been sure of Noah's guilt from the beginning and obviously still was.

'How did you find me?'

'Letters.'

'What do you mean – letters?'

'We'd given up hope of ever tracking you down when we started to receive letters. From someone who signs himself Lazarus. He thought that we might be interested to know your whereabouts in connection with your wife's death.'

So, Noah thought, this was Lazarus's way of preventing him from finding out the truth. He was getting the police to do his dirty work for him.

'You've got the wrong man,' Noah said.

'You say you're innocent. But don't you think you have compounded your guilt by running away from the scene of the crime?'

'I needed to prove my innocence.'

The street's tall, dark buildings shrouded in shadows reminded Noah of the urban desolation of an Edward Hopper painting.

'So you thought you would track down her murderer,' the detective asked. 'Perhaps find her body?'

'Yes.'

'Curiosity killed the cat. You should have left that kind of work to us.'

'How could I have, when you were so intent on finding me guilty?'

'Not necessarily. There are things about this Lazarus that puzzle us. He seems to have come out of nowhere. We can find no history of him. Just as we could find no history of Pandora. We think there must be some kind of connection between him and your wife. If she ever existed at all.'

'What on earth do you mean?'

'There is a mystery surrounding your wife's body, Dr Close. We searched your house and garden and there was no trace of it. In fact there were no signs that her body could have been carried out of the bedroom at all. No traces of blood or hair on the window or door or carpet. The only blood that left the room was on your hands, after you had touched her body.

'There is something else even more disturbing, Dr Close, that I have to tell you. The blood we tested on the walls and on the bed, within the room, was not of any human type. Nor of any animal or reptile. It was of a blood type not known to man.'

'You're telling me that Pandora wasn't real? Perhaps she's a creature from another planet. Or perhaps I *made her up?*' Noah made no attempt to keep the irony out of his voice. 'I'm not prepared to believe *that*. For where does that leave me?'

'I've no idea. Those are your suggestions, not mine.'

'So, if there's no evidence of a murder having taken place, why have you been following me? Stalking me down dark streets?'

'I was curious Dr Close. Just like you. I thought by following you I would find out what was really going on. But you are obviously in the dark as much as I am. What I do know is that you are a free man. You can return home whenever you wish. There are no records of your wife, no body, and her existence in the first place, let alone her death, now seems in doubt. I would now leave well alone.'

'I can't do that. Pandora was as real as you and I.'

'So you are prepared to risk your life? And perhaps other people's? Lazarus seems a dangerous man. Whatever his motives.'

Noah thought of Venus and hesitated, just for a moment. 'Yes I am. Knowledge isn't risk-free. I used to think it was. Not any more.'

The detective shook his head. 'It's up to you.'

He then turned and walked back down the street leaving Noah standing alone in the middle of the pavement. The detective's footsteps could be heard fading into the distance long after he had disappeared out of sight, round the corner.

Noah knew that only the truth would offer him respite, give him peace and serenity, the oneness he was looking for. It gave him a strange sense of power that the gift of serenity could lie in his hands. He may have been the instigator, the driver of this tension, but he could also be its liberator.

He knew that the secret to Pandora's death must lie inside the box. This time when he scaled the high white walls of Lazarus's garden, he was possessed by a strength that he did not know he had. He entered the unlocked door of the palace and walked through the main room, weaving through the sculptures' sepulchral presences, the moon shining down though the cupola in the ceiling. Having walked into the inner courtyard he at first thought that the stone statue of Pandora in the fountain had been painted in the garish colours of classical times.

But as he approached the statue, he recognised the vulnerable flesh and thin bones of a real body standing where the statue should have been. Venus stood there, rigid, as if her body had turned to stone. She was dressed as the statue of Pandora had been dressed, however her clothes were not made of clay but of soft fabric which clung to her, wet from the splashes of the fountain. Glass eyes had been put into her empty eye-sockets. Pandora's box had been wedged between her outstretched hands.

Noah did not feel anything at all as his life, up to this point, had now prepared him for everything. He walked through the water of the fountain, which came up to his waist in a cold embrace, hearing the rustle of the wind in the tree, a cool breeze in a hot night. The spray of the fountain was like crystals falling through the air.

He reached out and touched Venus' arm. He expected it to be cold, thinking she was dead, but her skin was warm. He felt her pulse and could sense a very faint beat: it was as if she had been frozen in time. A potion similar to the one he had been given in the warehouse, but much stronger, had paralysed her movements.

But even now his curiosity drove him forward, he still had to find out what lay inside Pandora's box. A sweet scent of lavender and roses emanated from Venus, as reaching up, he tried to wrest the box from her hands. Wrenching hard, in vain, Noah was becoming drenched in the cool water until it was running down his face. He peered up between Venus' hands and saw that nails had been bored through her palms into the metal bars that crossed the glass box.

He balanced on the plinth so that he was level with Venus and tried to open the lid to look inside. He could hear her heart beating. To his surprise the lid opened easily and he peered inside. Letting the lid fall shut again, Noah fell down into the fountain, on his knees, the water up to his neck and for the first time since Pandora's death he surrendered to grief. He wept, as if his heart was breaking.

Venus, from her pedestal stared out, sightless, over his head, as if she had known what he had discovered, all along. That she had known, all along, that the box would be empty.

The town was dark outside. It was like a dragon stirring, flexing its muscles with all those lights for eyes. Sometimes it went completely black, shut all its eyes, fell asleep, grew quiet. People climbed over its back between its limbs. This monster that they had created with its own momentum and its own effects. They were its scales. They were its sense of justice.

The air was dry like cotton swathed about Noah's mouth, drying out his mouth. Dry air that smeared him with its own ointment. There was no noise at night. The curfew had fallen, as Noah managed to drag Venus down from the plinth, pulling the nails from her rigid hands, and letting the box fall into the fountain. The box slowly spiralled through the water and came to rest at the bottom. He carried her out through the palace, opening the gates from the inside and dragging her through the streets. Hoisting her stiff arms around his neck, as if she were a drunk hanging on for dear life, he half carried, half pulled her up the stairs to their room, ripped off her tunic and put her to bed. She lay there inert. He climbed into bed next to her, closed her eyelids over her staring glass eyes, and embraced her with his arms. She had always been light in his arms, he remembered.

All his medical skills could not help Venus recover the use of her limbs. She lay there immobile in bed while he had to hope that nature would take its course, that the poison would run through her system. Her voice was the first thing to come back.

'What happened Venus?' Noah asked 'Why did he do it? Why did he blind you?'

'Because he wanted to stop my visions in case my gift returned. He wanted to stop me seeing the truth. He hasn't the imagination to realise that my visions have nothing to do with my eyes.'

He was struck by her coolness, her lack of emotion. All her interior resources, the interior world she had been living in, which had been stolen from her first by Las Vegas, then by Lazarus, had returned to become a source of strength.

Noah saw his chance: 'Doesn't what he's done to you prove that he, not I, killed Pandora? Otherwise why is he so frightened of your powers?'

'You're right Noah. I'm sorry that I believed what he was saying about you. I knew it would be dangerous for someone like me to get involved with Lazarus in the first place. But I had to, for your sake.'

However, Venus also had other information that, because she loved Noah, was information that she didn't want. What Venus did not say was that Lazarus had told her Noah was a doctor. Therefore her vision of seeing Pandora's neck slit by a surgeon's knife implicated Noah beyond the suspension of her belief.

All her life, Venus had had knowledge she didn't want.

Her psychic powers had been not a gift, but a curse. They had stopped her from living. Her imagination had paradoxically weighed her down with knowledge. The Future and Death had become the same for her. She was used to being in an unnatural state of awareness where spontaneous sensation was denied her. Her mind had been in paralysis, in the same way her body, now her gift had been lifted, was now unable to move. So keeping this new kind of knowledge to herself was not difficult, she had become an expert at living with pain.

Noah was oblivious to what was inside her mind, mistaking her introspection for concern for him. 'Don't worry, I will be safe, Venus. I will go into Lazarus's heart and find out the reason for Pandora's death. Find out where her body is so I can mourn her properly. I have a pragmatism to match his own.'

'But don't you see, imagination, even if it leaves you vulnerable, as it did me, is the only way you will find out the truth?'

Noah dreamt of feeling his bones crush and crumble beneath the sliding layer of skin. Of his body gently folding like an origami bird.

He found Lazarus at the gaming table, running risks and always winning. Lazarus looked up and smiled at him, as if he had been expecting him. The atmosphere was intense. Lazarus always did this to the atmosphere. Burnt it up, made it difficult to breathe. He liked to suffocate the air.

'Did you know that in Greek, to seduce also means to destroy? They understood about life, then.' Lazarus motioned with his hand. 'Come and sit down beside me, Noah. You wanted to know if I knew Pandora? A fair enough concern for any husband. The answer is I knew her as well as anyone knows anyone, perhaps just that little bit more.

'But she was an act of your creation wasn't she, Noah? You forged her from fire. How can you expect loyalty from a phantom of your own imagination? Chimeras have needs of their own, take on a life of their own, wreak havoc if forced to tow the line.

'You created your own monster, Dr Close. Just as the Greeks created their gods. Gods who then walked the earth like mortals, causing more trouble than any man could have dreamed of. Just for fun.'

But Noah would not be distracted from pinning Lazarus down. 'So it was you who wrote the words on your gate, DO NOT BE AFRAID OF WHAT YOU WANT, on pieces of paper and sent them to her.'

'That's right – in a manner of speaking. I felt responsible for setting her free.'

139

'Free from what?'

'Free from your definition of her. It's hard work being a goddess, god knows. Perhaps she wanted a change. A metamorphosis of some kind.'

Noah was growing impatient with Lazarus's tangents. 'But if you wanted her free, why did you murder her?'

'But I keep on telling you. I didn't.'

'So who did. What are you saying? *That I murdered my own wife?* Why do you keep on saying this? Are you trying to drive me mad?'

As Noah said the words, he felt dizzy on adrenaline and disbelief, a euphoria of disconnectedness with what was happening to him. He watched the wheel going round and round, his mind becoming as blurred as the ball that seemed to be disappearing into thin air.

Had he killed Pandora? It suddenly seemed blindingly apparent to Noah that it was a possibility, a possibility which up to now he might have blocked out. He felt as if he were going mad with an idea that his imagination couldn't decipher. But he also knew that he had to get through this in order to reach the other end, in order to find out the truth. But *why? Why* should he have killed Pandora? He had nothing but love for her, loved her to the point, where he had no longer seen her as mortal.

That night Noah dreamt that Pandora came to him

while he was sleeping. He opened his eyes as he felt her warm, naked body slipping into the bed beside him. She was even more voluptuous than he had remembered her, and as he bent down over her breasts, he could not restrain himself from taking a bite out of her full flesh, of feeling her blood fill up his mouth. He swallowed a mouthful of her body as she lay there smiling, waiting for him to finish what he had started.

Noah started to follow Lazarus more closely, this time he followed him not only to his home but inside it. He had the feeling all along that Lazarus knew what he was doing, how Noah was watching him. Now Noah watched him not only take women home but also undress them. They stood suddenly naked in the centre of the room under the light, as if they had shed their skins. Was Lazarus in love with any of these women? Surely love was outside his sphere? It seemed blasphemous to think of Lazarus suffering the metamorphosis of love.

Perhaps he had not given Pandora love, but her voice back instead, a voice of quick-silver words that Lazarus would have heard for the first time.

Noah found himself thinking about Lazarus incessantly – he was becoming preoccupied, his imagination fired up. What was this pull that Lazarus had over him? He had never come across anything like it, except with Pandora. He could not make sense of it.

Noah began to feel when he was with Lazarus a change in perspective took place. That finding the proof that Lazarus was his wife's killer, finding out what he had done to her body, was not quite so important. What was important was to be in Lazarus's company. To feel like oneself again, to feel risen from the dead.

Venus was slowly regaining the use of her limbs. Although blinded she seemed to have a vague vision, like a third eye, that allowed her to make out shapes and forms surprisingly clearly.

'I'm being haunted by the devil,' he said to Venus. 'He keeps on getting inside my head.'

'We'll exorcise him,' she said. She tied Noah to the bed. He lay there awake, looking at the ceiling, sweating. He saw the devil hanging over him, reaching out his hands to him.

Venus sat by him, stroking him, wiping the sweat from him, calming his screams.

'You are possessed,' she said. 'Possessed by him. We'll have to leave. You are just a home for him. Somewhere to stay.' She drained the blood from him. Took a knife and marked him. Burnt the soles and palms of his feet.

The city always looked as if the earth below it was about to open and it would disappear into it. The neon lights from the casinos reflected in Venus' eyes, turned her glass irises red.

Noah realised that the power of Lazarus lay in his blankness, his inscrutability. It allowed other people to imagine who he was. His blankness was a form of manipulation. The power he had was in direct proportion to the weakness of his victims. Noah knew that he couldn't leave the city yet. Lazarus was playing with, manipulating his imagination, allowing him fantasies that suggested that he, Noah, was a murderer and that Lazarus was not mortal.

Noah didn't know a way round this except to prove that his own imagination was wrong.

The Chinese say, that the moment you want to win, that is the moment you are defeated. Lazarus drew strength from the weakness inherent in those who wanted to win. He turned their desire into a fatal flaw until the victim began to eat his own tail. He allowed his victims to do all the hard work themselves. Lazarus was nothing without his victims and he needed them in order to be born again.

*

Noah decided to break into Lazarus's house to find out, by force if necessary, the truth from Lazarus himself, to stop up the insidious fantasies that were crowding reason out of his head. This time when Noah tried to open the mirrored door it was locked, and he had to smash the door with his fist, the glass splintering around him and shattering his reflection in the dusk. He entered the main room and to his surprise all the sculptures had gone. The only thing that stood in the room was his reflection. There was nowhere for Noah to hide.

Noah went into the inner courtyard where the fountain was playing. In the twilight shadow of the inner courtyard, Lazarus was standing, waiting for him.

'I've decided to leave this place,' Lazarus said.

'Not before you tell me why you killed Pandora.'

'Curiosity killed the cat.'

'At least tell me what you have done with her body?'

'The body of a woman is a beautiful thing. A work of art. Like one of my sculptures.'

Noah seized Lazarus and dragged him over to the fountain where Venus had once stood holding the box. He put Lazarus's head over the water and took out his surgeon's knife from his pocket and put it against his neck.

'Are you telling me you carved sculptures out of her bone? Do you *want* me to kill you?'

Lazarus looked up at him, completely unconcerned and said quietly, Noah's knife still hard up against his neck, 'Isn't that your reason for being here? Perhaps if you hadn't been so fearful of your own imagination you would have managed to sort out fancy from fact. Then you wouldn't need to do what you are about to do.'

Noah, further angered, tightened his hands around Lazarus's head and pushed it under the water. Lazarus's hair flowed out around him and Noah was suddenly disturbed by his memory of Venus' vision of Pandora floating under water. Lazarus did not struggle, he seemed serene, his face smiling up, as if through glass. Noah expertly slit Lazarus's throat. He held him under water until the water of the fountain grew dark with his blood.

Noah lay down on the ground, his head against the rim of the fountain, and curled up beside the prone body of Lazarus and watched the sky blacken until he fell asleep. When he woke up the body of Lazarus had disappeared. Only a pile of his clothes remained in a heap beside the fountain.

Traces of wet footprints crossed the inner courtyard's floor, from where the body had lain. Noah noticed that Lazarus's wet footprints had six toes. The prints of the feet began the size of a man's foot but as they progressed across the floor they grew smaller and narrower transforming gradually into the shape of a woman's feet. Noah followed the footprints out of the garden but they stopped abruptly in the courtyard under the starlit sky.

Noah never talked of what had happened in the courtyard of Lazarus's palace, but after he returned to the hotel to collect Venus to leave town, she knew that they were on the run again, that she had thrown in her lot with him.

Noah and Venus, after weeks of driving, finally found themselves driving up a long, rough, track which wound its way up a mountain. At the end of the track stood a small, wooden shack, an old shepherd's home, with nothing but two rooms and the most basic amenities. They decided to make it their home.

In this barren place, it snowed heavily in the winter and the sun blistered down during the summer, the extremity of the weather compensating for the exhaustion of their emotions. Waterfalls fell down over the ruinous rocks and hawks swooped down low at dusk.

They were self-sufficient, living off what they managed to grow in the dry soil and the animals they trapped. Venus' eyesight slowly continued to improve, but they both knew that they would have to be patient

and simply wait, before she fully regained her indepen-
dence.

For a while Venus and Noah lived in the shadow of what
had happened to them. They spent much of their time in
silence, gradually growing used to each other's touch.
They would walk through the forest that grew below their
home, the light shining through the leaves to the darkness
beneath.

Noah would lead Venus through the path that wound
its way across the forest floor. She could now see almost
perfectly in daylight, but still had trouble making forms
out after dusk fell. But it was then that her lost visions
became strongest, ghosts of images rearing up, but then
dissipating quickly again, much to her relief.

Now that Venus had lost her visions, a sense of spon-
taneity and hope had returned. She no longer had the gift
of prophecy, could no longer see clues to the future, to her
death. Instead she was aware of the touch of the world
around her. She had known what Death was like, her
imagination had managed to look into its eyes, but she
had chosen life. It was not that she did not understand that
Death still lay at the centre of life – she did not, could
forget – but this understanding no longer prevented
from living. When Venus looked to the future now, she

not see a series of set images, painted on to glass, but a play of shadow and light.

Noah and Venus never fully came out from under the shadow of their past: it would not have been possible, but the patches of light on the forest floor were something they both noticed now.

ABOUT THE AUTHOR

Alice Thompson studied English at Oxford University. Her first novel, *Justine*, was joint winner of the James Tait Black Memorial Prize for fiction, Scotland's oldest literary prize. She is currently a writer in residence at St. Andrew's University.